She Could Never Win Against This Man

"I despise you!" Alex flashed at him.

"Do you indeed?" Damon moved slowly toward her. "What you need, little girl, is to be taken firmly in hand, and I'm just the man for the job."

Alex turned to get away from him, but a hand reached out to grab her wrist. Even as she tried to free herself, she felt a shock of excitement course up her arm. She was stunned by the sensation. Surely she wasn't attracted to this man?

Her eyes met his, but she couldn't read his expression. The anger had retreated, but it had left nothing in its place.

BRENDA TRENT
has a life right out of romance. She followed her heart from Virginia to California, where she met and married the man of her dreams. With his encouragement she gave up working to concentrate on another dream: writing. We are proud to introduce her work through Silhouette Romances.

Dear Reader:

Silhouette Romances is an exciting new publishing venture. We will be presenting the very finest writers of contemporary romantic fiction as well as outstanding new talent in this field. It is our hope that our stories, our heroes and our heroines will give you, the reader, all you want from romantic fiction.

Also, *you* play an important part in our future plans for Silhouette Romances. We welcome any suggestions or comments on our books and I invite you to write to us at the address below.

So, enjoy this book and all the wonderful romances from Silhouette. They're for *you!*

Karen Solem
Editor-in-Chief
Silhouette Books
P.O. Box 769
New York, N.Y. 10019

BRENDA TRENT
Winter Dreams

Silhouette *Romance*
Published by Silhouette Books New York
America's Publisher of Contemporary Romance

To Ellen,
June and Kathy

Other Silhouette Romances by Brenda Trent

Rising Star

SILHOUETTE BOOKS, a Simon & Schuster Division of
GULF & WESTERN CORPORATION
1230 Avenue of the Americas, New York, N Y 10020

ISBN: 0-671-57074-9

First Silhouette printing April, 1981

10 9 8 7 6 5 4 3 2 1

America's Publisher of Contemporary Romance

Printed in the U.S.A.

Chapter One

In the bright sun of a January California day, the petite
blond trudged up the steps of the plane and smiled
vaguely at the stewardess who welcomed her aboard.
Attempting to hide her unhappiness, Alex found her
seat and settled in. She raised her hand to her forehead,
rested her elbow on the armrest, and stared out the
window, waiting for the plane to depart.

Her grief over her mother's death was still fresh and
painful, and her own confusion and uncertainty left
Alex shaken. She would give anything, she told herself,
not to have promised her mother she would go to
Willowstone to live with Damon Montaigne. Sighing
again, she blinked back the tears building in her wide
blue eyes. It was ridiculous! Damon Montaigne of all
people! How could her mother have asked her to have
any dealings with the man at all, let alone go live with
him? Her face creased with displeasure. She hadn't
seen him since she was ten years old. He was a stranger
to her now, and that was just the way she wanted it to
stay. Although he was her father's former business
partner, his name was shrouded with mystery and
tainted with slander. The split between the two men
had so embittered her father that he had never been
able to tell her what had happened. He had refused any

contact with Damon after leaving Virginia ten years before, and Alex certainly didn't want anything to do with him now.

She struggled to recall the man's face, but it was useless. She just didn't remember his features. She had only the faintest memory of him as a towering giant who had fallen into grave disfavor. Her recollection of him only made her mother's request seem all the more peculiar.

Her mother's last words echoed in her head. "Damon has made a success of the secretarial schools and he's wealthy now. He knows our situation and he wants you to share his home."

Alex was aghast. "Mother, you can't expect me to—"

"Alex, don't be difficult. I haven't done right by you. I should have given you so much more. This is the only way I have to make it up to you."

"I'll be fine, Mother," Alex assured her, trying to hide the tears that were threatening to fall. "I can make my own way."

"But you don't need to, Alex. Damon wants to put you through college. Let him do it. There's no reason for you to try to work and struggle through school. The insurance money from your father is gone, and I know how much you want your education. It wasn't fair for you to have to drop out to care for me."

"Mother, I wanted to care for you," Alex murmured. "I was only in my second semester."

"But you'd already changed your mind about your career once, and you haven't even had a chance to try out this new choice you've made. What do you really know about being a veterinarian? In a lot of ways you're a dreamer like your father, Alex. You don't realize how much he sheltered you and influenced you. Oh, I'd feel so much better about you if you would go to Damon. You've never been completely alone."

"I changed my mind about teaching because I

realized the field is overcrowded. I won't change my mind again, and I'll pay my own way."

"Alex, please! Don't let me die before you agree to this request. I want you to start life with some advantages. At least give this a try. Promise me you'll stay with Damon until you're twenty-one."

Despite Alex's determination, a tear escaped her eye and fell from her long lashes. There was no way, in clear conscience, that she could have refused her mother's last request, no matter how foolish it seemed to her or how bitterly she objected to it. But she was desperately unhappy about it; she would rather have been given any other choice.

As the tear trickled down her face, she brushed angrily at it with her hand. She had wanted to remain in California. She was twenty years old and she felt that it was absurd to go live with a stranger. And especially this stranger. She didn't trust the man for a moment; his sudden interest in her career smacked of insincerity. There was more to it than met the eye, but her mother had been too ill to realize that, and Alex hadn't been able to convince her of it. What was really behind his sudden willingness to put her through college? It seemed a bit late for generosity. And why did he want her to live in his house?

Regardless of his reasons, Alex wanted no part of him. In four months she would be twenty-one. Once she had kept her part of the agreement, she wouldn't stay with Damon a moment longer. She would find a job and put herself through school. She was thankful that she had worked in an animal shelter for two summers; at least she wasn't totally without work experience. The lengthy time she had spent caring for her mother had left her with few opportunities to pursue either a social life or career plans. Alex didn't know how they would have lived if it hadn't been for the insurance money they had received when her father died.

While they were struggling for every penny, Damon had lived in luxury. The thought of him caused a fresh surge of anger to rise in Alex. She detested the man already, and she wouldn't stay in his home any longer than she had to. He had cheated her father somehow, she was sure. A thought that had been circling for some time in her mind finally took hold. She would get to the bottom of the reason for her parents' hasty flight to California. She would find out what had happened between Damon Montaigne and her father. The idea made her trip a little more tolerable, and she leaned back in her seat, concentrating on the situation.

So lost was she in her thoughts that she hardly realized that the plane was taking off. In no time, it seemed, dinner had been served and the plane was landing in Georgia, where she would transfer to a smaller aircraft for the final leg of her trip.

The distance from Atlanta to Danville, Virginia, seemed short, and Alex's heart dropped abruptly as the plane began to descend. She barely remembered the town, and the prospect of "going home" was anything but pleasant. As hard as she tried, she couldn't recall anything about Damon Montaigne's appearance except his size. She wondered how she was supposed to recognize him. When he had spoken with her on the phone, he had briskly assured her that there would be no problem. Anxiety and resentment rose in her at the idea of meeting him face to face.

A small, fortyish, gray-haired man sedately dressed in brown slacks, a light gray pullover sweater, and a dark brown coat called out her name as she walked into the small terminal. "Miss Hawthorne? Miss Hawthorne?" His manner was meek and she hadn't expected him to look so old.

"Yes, Mr. Montaigne." She tried to keep the surprise out of her voice. She had understood that Damon had been quite young when he went into business with her father. She hadn't expected him to be more than thirty-one now.

"Oh, I'm not Mr. Montaigne," the man drawled apologetically, peering over his glasses at her. "Mr. Montaigne was detained by business, so he sent me in his stead. I'm George Willis. Please wait here and I'll get your baggage."

Even though Alex gave him a brief smile, she was seething with resentment and burning with indignation. Damon Montaigne didn't seem very eager to welcome her. If he couldn't even bother to meet her at the airport himself, why had he wanted her to come at all? Was he fulfilling what he considered to be his obligation to his former partner by taking in his impoverished offspring? And why should he feel any obligation? Was it guilt? Or something else? She knew that Damon, as the younger partner in the business venture, had invested some money, but she also knew that the secretarial school had been her father's dream. After he left Danville, all of his later ventures had resulted in dismal failure. Was Mr. Montaigne salving his conscience because he had succeeded with her father's dream while her father had lost everything? Wasn't it a little late for remorse?

Well, she had no intention of being used to mitigate his guilt. And if he were the least bit inhospitable, she would find a job in town and manage for herself. She didn't need him. Since her father's death and her mother's illness, she had taken care of herself, and she still could. This was her mother's idea; she certainly wouldn't have accepted his charity otherwise.

George Willis appeared with her bags, struggling with the one Alex had filled with her favorite books. "Here we are, Miss Hawthorne," he said quietly. "Are you ready to go?"

"Of course," she snapped, venting her anger toward Damon Montaigne on George Willis. Ashamed of her sharpness, she added, "It was so nice of you to be here when I arrived. I was concerned that no one would come for me—or that I wouldn't recognize whoever *did* come."

George smiled with thin lips. "Oh, Mr. Montaigne wouldn't have left you stranded. He's quite serious about his responsibilities."

His responsibilities! Alex fumed. Already she was Damon Montaigne's responsibility, and she hadn't even seen him in ten years! Just who did he think he was dealing with? She was an adult, and she would let him know in a hurry that he needn't feel responsible for her!

Darkness had already settled in when she and George got to Willowstone, but from what Alex could see of it under the colonial lamps it was truly magnificent. An old Southern mansion, it stood proud and stately in the dim light of the ancient gold lamp posts. Even though her mother had said Damon Montaigne was wealthy, Alex hadn't been prepared for such splendor. The grounds appeared extensive; shadowy stands of trees were barely visible in the darkness, making the house look as if it were in a forest.

Alex's heart hammered a little when George opened the door of the car for her, took out her luggage, and escorted her up the winding walk. Suddenly she wished she had taken time to powder her nose; she always felt that her freckles made her look young, and that was the very last thing she wanted Damon Montaigne to think she was. She felt ridiculous being in this position as it was.

She tried to still her beating heart when George rang the doorbell and stepped back to await an answer. Because the backward step seemed defensive, she had to force her own feet to stay still. After all, she didn't know what to expect from the man. He had dealt unfairly with her father, and she had no idea what he was capable of. Shivering slightly, she was unsure if she was cold or just apprehensive. Almost immediately a short, stout woman appeared in the massive doorway.

"Well, well! If it isn't little Alexandria all grown up!" she exclaimed. Alex was taken aback by the woman's Southern drawl, which was even more pronounced than George Willis's because of the loudness of her voice. Her own parents had originally spoken in the distinct Southern manner, but as time passed their accents had lessened, and Alex herself spoke as a Californian with no trace of Southern heritage.

"How do you do?" Alex extended a rigid hand. She had no memory of the heavy, brightly dressed woman who so obviously had known her as a child.

"Well, don't just stand there, honey. Come on in. Bring that luggage inside, George," the woman said. Alex stepped into a beautiful, wide central hall decorated with Ben Franklin chairs and an elegant, leggy settee. Abruptly, the woman hugged Alex. "Well, you didn't get very tall, but you sure got pretty—just like your mama, aren't you?"

Though Alex felt a dull ache of sadness at the mention of her mother, she carefully concealed her unhappiness. "Thank you," she replied politely.

"Don't you remember ol' Letti?" A broad smile lit the heavy features. "I'm Damon's housekeeper. Your ma and pa used to bring you out to visit when the Montaignes had the old farm. You were a little one and pretty as a doll you were. 'Course, I was a lot smaller myself then," she added good-naturedly. "Well, now, don't be shy. You come on. Let's go get you reacquainted with Damon."

Taking Alex by the hand, the woman pulled her along the polished hallway beautifully highlighted by large hanging lamps. She opened a door to the right and entered a lovely dining room, which featured a massive stone fireplace. Alex glanced at a lovely chandelier, and then her eyes settled nervously on the dark, broodingly handsome man sitting at the large table. It certainly didn't look like he had been detained from picking her up at the airport because of business, she thought irritably.

"Here she is, Damon," Letti announced proudly, pulling Alex forward as if she were a wayward child. Alex's shoes made a heavy noise on the shining wood floor. The sound was magnified in the quiet room, and Alex had an absurd impulse to walk on tiptoe in the overpowering presence of Damon Montaigne. She could feel her heart pounding furiously inside her breast. "You remember Damon, honey?" Letti asked.

"How do you do, Mr. Montaigne?" Alex murmured, feeling ridiculous as she stood before the silent man. His failure to respond immediately angered her; impulsively, she snapped, "I see you've finished with your business."

Damon took a long draw on a sleek black pipe before removing it from his mouth. His dark, smoldering eyes gave her a careful appraisal, and his lips twitched in a suppressed smile as he continued to survey her.

"Yes, Miss Hawthorne," he agreed. "And I see that you've arrived safely." His gaze flickered over her clothes. "How was your trip? I didn't expect to see you dressed as a little boy. Did you arrive by horse?"

Alex's eyes shot to her blue jeans and checkered blue shirt; it was her usual California costume, and she had wanted to travel in comfort. Her eyes rested on the pointed toes of her brown cowboy boots, currently in high fashion, and she stood straighter to increase her small stature. Forcing her eyes back to Damon, she glared angrily at him. He was still staring at her boots, and his face wore a barely controlled look of amusement. Alex jerked her blue jacket tightly to her body and tilted her head.

"I'm not dressed as a little boy, Mr. Montaigne," she flared haughtily. "I can see that you don't know much about women's fashions—or their ages. I'm twenty years old, in case you don't know it. A woman!"

Really, she fumed, he was the most insufferable man she'd ever met!

Damon's devilishly handsome face broke into a slight smile. With the taunting look of a man who had unexpectedly discovered a fascinating game, he announced, "Well, so you are, Miss Hawthorne. So you are. Please, sit down. We've been waiting dinner for you." He gestured to the chair nearest him.

"You shouldn't have," Alex retorted, annoyed by his remark about her outfit. She hadn't come all this way to have him make snide comments about her clothes. Obstinately, she remained where she was. "I have no intention of putting you to any trouble." She disliked the man already, and she knew that she had been extremely foolish to come here. She could certainly understand her father's aversion to him. Feeling unnaturally cross, she added, "Of course, I doubt that I will be putting you to any trouble. You certainly didn't trouble yourself to meet me at the airport." The minute she had said them, the words sounded terribly rude to her, but it was too late to retract them.

Damon's full dark eyebrows arched up as he watched her speculatively. "Have I hurt your feelings already, Miss Hawthorne? I'm sure George explained that I had business. I just finished a few minutes ago. However," he added with a hint of a smile, "I'm pleased that you've no wish to trouble me. I'll store that remark away for future reference. And I do like to have everyone sit down to dinner on time. It's one of my little quirks." The expression on his face was perfectly calm, and Alex's fury rose.

"I've no doubt that you have many little quirks, Mr. Montaigne," she snapped.

"Now, Damon, don't tease," Letti interrupted. "Alexandria is bound to be tired."

With easy movements, Damon laid down his pipe and pushed back his chair to stand at the head of the table. Alex's breath caught in her throat. She had to admit that he was dashingly handsome—at least six feet tall with dark, virile looks. A scarlet sweater hugged his massive chest, emphasizing broad shoulders; beige slacks outlined his muscled thighs and slim hips. He sauntered toward Alex while she watched him with wary blue eyes.

"Of course you're tired, my dear," he murmured with disarming concern. "Let me help you out of your jacket." Before Alex could step away or protest, he tugged at the tailored material as he towered over her. Removing the jacket, he thrust it at Letti, then directed Alex to a chair and seated her before she could gather her wits. Anger was flaming inside her; there was no reason for the man's insufferable behavior. He was treating her like a child. She was beginning to dislike him more with each passing second.

Trying to regain her composure, she stared down at the elegant place setting. His mansion and his money might put him in the position of ordering other people around, but he wouldn't succeed with her with those tactics. After all, she knew that his glory had been achieved at the expense of her father's dream. And if he pushed her too far, she would tell him so!

"I'll help you with the food, Letti," Damon said. "Let's get dinner on the table."

Alex watched Letti and Damon disappear through the swinging door, and she clenched her fists unconsciously. Who did he think he was, anyway? She would like to find some proof of his underhanded dealings with her father. She would love to be the one to take him down a peg or two. He was unbelievably arrogant! She forced herself to breathe slowly and look around at the beauty of her surroundings. Trying to ignore the low voices coming from the kitchen as the swinging door continued its back and forth movement, she concentrated on the fireplace, but she couldn't help overhearing Letti's overloud whisper.

"Show some respect for that girl's grief, Damon

Montaigne. I raised you with more manners than you're showing, I declare I did. What's got into you?''

Damon's deep voice was almost painfully clear. "She has to put her grief behind her now, Letti. Life goes on. I know she's had a rough time of it, but now I want her to concentrate on the future.''

Alex fought down the urge to march into the kitchen and give him a piece of her mind. What did he know about her grief? What did he care?

Their voices faded as they approached the swinging door. Letti entered first, laden with a tray of covered dishes. Damon followed with a large platter that held a beautiful, honey-glazed ham topped with pineapple slices and Bing cherries.

Hunger rapidly obscured Alex's anger as she watched the food being spread out on the table. Tempting mounds of whipped potatoes topped with melting yellow butter, green peas with tiny pearl onions, cranberry sauce, and golden fluffy biscuits set her taste buds tingling. A week had gone by since she had eaten properly and she focused all her attention on the food that was passed to her. When she had filled her plate, she waited for Damon to fill his. She was mildly surprised to see Letti sit down to dinner with them, but apparently the older woman was considered part of the family. After Letti served herself, Alex picked up her fork to take a bite of the tantalizing potatoes.

Her appetite undaunted by her unpleasant meeting with her host, she ate with enthusiasm, responding politely to Letti's conversation. However, she refused to carry on any communication with Damon beyond what was absolutely necessary. Abiding by her mother's peculiar wish, she would live in his home until she was twenty-one, but there was nothing in the agreement that said she had to like the supercilious Mr. Montaigne. She was aware of his dark eyes on her throughout the meal and she answered his pointed questions as concisely as possible, but she rarely did him the courtesy of looking at him when he spoke. It was only too obvious that she had been insane to agree to her mother's request, but how could she have done otherwise at the time?

When Letti excused herself to get dessert and coffee, an awkward silence settled in the room. Even Letti must have felt the chill when she returned because she broke into instant chatter as she set down a delectable-looking concoction. "Homemade persimmon pudding with hot lemon sauce," she said. "The persimmons came right off our own trees. Have you ever tasted persimmon pudding, Alex?"

"Not that I recall."

"It's a winter fruit," Letti explained. "The fruit ripens in November or thereabouts, but a frost has to bite it before it's ready for the picking. If it's picked too soon, it's bitter."

The frost must never have bitten Damon, as bitter as he is, Alex thought, but she murmured, "How interesting."

Finding the dessert delicious, she was tempted to ask for a second helping, but abruptly Damon stood up. "Letti will show you to your rooms, Miss Hawthorne."

Alex had had about all of his high-handed treatment that she could stand. She opened her mouth to say she wasn't ready to go to her room yet, but Letti spoke before she could.

"Really, Damon," Letti insisted, frowning, "I'm sure you can call her Alexandria."

The dark glint in Damon's eyes yielded to a look of feigned despair. "But, Letti, Miss Hawthorne hasn't given me permission to address her so casually, and apparently I'm not in the know when it comes to—young women. I don't want to make another error like the first one concerning her clothes."

Alex directed a brief, withering smile toward Damon before turning to Letti. "Please call me Alex," she said.

"All right then, Alex," Damon said, ignoring the fact

that she hadn't spoken to him. "Letti will still show you to your rooms. George has already brought your luggage up. Please let me know if you need or want anything. I trust the rooms will be satisfactory."

"Thank you," Alex replied with asperity, not bothering to look at him as she followed Letti from the room. She was angry at the way Damon had dismissed her so summarily and, looking for excuses to defy him, she asked, "Can't I help you with the dishes before I go to my room, Letti?"

"Oh, no, honey. You're bound to be tired. We're going to put you in the room that used to belong to Damon's mother. It's a real nice room. You get yourself settled in."

When Letti walked up the gleaming stairway, Alex trailed behind, sliding her hand on the magnificent ornate bannister. Trying to think of anything but the way Damon angered her, she paused at the landing to look down on the hall, and she couldn't help but wonder how many rooms the mansion had. Damon Montaigne had done rather well with the money he had earned from her father's dream.

As though reading Alex's mind, Letti said, "There are seventeen rooms here in Willowstone. Damon had it remodeled several years ago when his mother died, may her soul rest in peace. The outside has been kept in its rightful state as much as possible except for additions. The house was built just before the Civil War and actually housed Confederate officers when Danville became the 'Last Capital of the Confederacy.' Willowstone has quite a history."

"How fascinating," Alex responded, brightening a little. "I'm a history buff and I had no idea Danville was important in the Civil War."

"Oh, yes, indeed. During the war this little town was a quartermaster's depot, a central rail center, and a prison camp for the Yankees. It was a hospital for the Confederate wounded, too. Jeff Davis and the Confederate government set up a temporary capital in Major W. T. Sutherlin's home." Pride was evident in Letti's voice. "You'll find this town right remarkable if you check into it. Why, we had the first municipal electric power plant in the whole United States right here in our city."

When Letti opened the door to the bedroom, Alex gasped. It was stunning. A massive floor-to-ceiling window was covered by pale pink brocade draperies. An elegant, dark wood bed was canopied with the same pale hues and covered with a pink satin coverlet that suggested cozy comfort. Plush Persian rugs in bright colors adorned the polished hardwood floor. Delicate magnolia-patterned wallpaper, highlighted by a fire dancing in a large brick fireplace, accented the room. What appeared to be a dressing screen carried the same fragile magnolia imprint. A stately colonial wardrobe, a high-backed velvet-seated chair, and a rolltop desk completed the decor. Looking at the room, Alex almost felt as if she had been cast back in time. It seemed that she had only to open the wardrobe to see the long skirts and lacy bonnets of the ladies of America's past.

"Here's your bath," Letti told her with a lift of her hand, drawing Alex back to the present. The vast bathroom Letti indicated featured a large sunken tub of marble. Turning, Letti walked to a louvered closet door. "Want me to help you hang your things?"

Alex shook her head, causing her silken blond hair to fall toward her face. "No, thank you, Letti. I can do it."

"Do you like the room?" Letti asked, her dark eyes bright.

An unbidden laugh escaped Alex's lips. "Oh, Letti, it's the most beautiful room I've ever been in."

Letti smiled. "Damon will be happy you like it. He wants you to make yourself right at home. And you let me know if you want anything. My rooms are right across from yours; Damon's are at the right at the head of the stairs." A frown crossed the woman's face. "Honey, I just want you to know how happy I am that you came. I didn't think I'd ever see your pretty face again. My heart was heavy when your father—" Her words stopped abruptly, and she waved her hand. "Heavens above, all that doesn't matter now. You sleep tight." She quickly stepped out of the room, shutting the door behind her.

Alex stood very still, watching the door close. She longed to run after Letti and ask her what she had intended to say. Apparently Letti knew what had happened between her father and Damon. She sighed. She didn't want to upset the housekeeper by pressing her on the subject. It was obvious Letti didn't want to say any more, so it would just have to wait until a more opportune time.

Shaking her head to clear it of the troubling subject, Alex waited until she heard Letti's steps fade, then she moved about the room savoring every detail as she ran her hands across the smooth varnish of the wood and caressed the lushness of the fabrics. Willowstone was a sharp contrast to the drab four-room house she and her mother had occupied. Spontaneously, she hugged her arms to her body, whirling about the room in delight. Then she stepped behind the dainty dressing screen and peered over the top, pretending for just a moment that she was disrobing for some ardent lover. Finally, with a smile, she went to the elegant bath to start her bath water. While the tub was filling, she slipped out of her boots, slacks, and shirt. Unlocking her suitcase, she removed her chenille robe and a nightgown and took them to the bathroom. Tomorrow she could put her things away. She had just unhooked her bra and started to slide the straps down her arms when she heard a knock on her door. Clutching her bra to her body and grabbing frantically for her shirt, she murmured, "Just a minute."

But before she could cover her nakedness, Damon stepped boldly into the room.

Alex couldn't believe it! With no regard for her request, he had barged right into the room! Desperate, she headed for cover behind the delicate dressing screen, but as she reached it she tripped over one of the boots she had carelessly discarded on the floor in front of the screen. Grasping wildly at the fragile screen, she felt it topple forward. She clung to it with one hand and to her bra and shirt with the other before she lost her grip on her clothes and fell forward on top of the screen. Lying there burning with shame, clad only in her panties and feeling like an utter fool, she looked up at Damon and accused, "I told you, 'Just a minute.'"

Before she could think straight, she was gently lifted up by strong hands and set on her feet. Her face flamed with embarrassment as she stared up into Damon's face. She was acutely aware of her seminaked state, and it was painfully obvious that he was aware of it too. His eyes roved hungrily over her body, taking in her full breasts and her sensual hips covered only by the sheer, lacy panties. Then his eyes moved to her shapely legs. Outraged by his brazen scrutiny, Alex knew she should protest, but she was hypnotized by his nearness. He seemed to have a strange power over her, and she felt her skin tingle under his bold gaze. Her heart was beating wildly, and it wasn't until he spoke that the spell was broken.

"Are you all right?" he murmured in a husky voice.

"I said 'Just a minute' when you knocked," she repeated hoarsely.

His hand reached out to brush her hair away from her face and, not knowing what he was going to do next, but feeling her heart pound beneath her exposed breasts, Alex knocked his hand away and covered herself with her hands. "How dare you try to take advantage of me!" she rasped at last. "Is this what you brought me here for? Don't you ever touch me again!"

Damon's eyes hardened, and his face became a cold mask. "Excuse me. I didn't know you weren't dressed and I didn't hear you tell me to wait when I knocked. I want to talk to you."

"Talk!" she cried, turning her back and quickly yanking on her shirt. "I'm hardly dressed to talk and, really, Mr. Montaigne, are you sure that's what you had on your mind? Couldn't your 'talk' have waited until morning?"

His eyes flicked over her once more, then, his face darkening ominously, Damon turned on his heel and strode out of her room, leaving a shocked, near-naked Alex to stare after him. He had behaved as if invading her privacy and humiliating her were nothing! And she—she had just stood there while he looked her up and down! She had found his nearness disturbing in ways she had never expected. He had made her feel— She resolutely pushed him from her mind.

Still trembling, Alex ran to the tub. The water had reached the top and she quickly turned off the taps. Taking a deep breath of relief that the situation wasn't any worse, she slipped out of her panties and shirt. With shaking hands, she piled her blond hair high on her head and slid into the warm water.

Her mind was in turmoil as she soaked. What had she let herself in for by coming here? Did Damon mean to make her his mistress in exchange for room and board? Had that been his plan all along? And her mother had said he was interested in her career! Well, if he thought he was going to seduce her, he had another thought coming! The next time he'd get slapped for his trouble. The nerve of him! Had he really not heard her reply, or had it been his intent to catch her unawares? She pondered the problem for a long time before she emerged and dried her flushed body with a rose-colored towel. Wearily, she stepped into her nightie and crawled into the luxurious bed, but her gaze shot nervously to the door. Was she safe sleeping here?

Hadn't Damon shown that he couldn't be trusted by charging in on her like that? She scooted out of bed and searched the door for a lock.

Darn! She should have known there wouldn't be one. Not knowing what else to do, she dragged the dressing screen in front of the door. She would make sure he didn't catch her unaware again. If Damon opened the door against the screen, she was sure to hear it. Slipping back into bed, she snuggled deeply under the covers. What a horrid man this Damon Montaigne was. And yet . . . and yet she had felt a wild excitement when he stood so near her. She had never known another sensation quite like it. She shivered at the memory and tried to suppress it. After all, she didn't care for him at all. Her mind whirling with thoughts of the master of Willowstone, she fell into a deep slumber.

Chapter Two

The noisy fussing of two blue jays on the windowsill awakened her. She gazed about at her lovely surroundings for just a moment before memories of last night jogged her senses and caused the color to rush to her face. She didn't know if she could look him in the eyes again. On the other hand, she couldn't avoid him forever. Frowning, she recalled that he had said he didn't hear her tell him to wait. Was it the truth? What would have happened if she hadn't knocked his hands away? If Damon couldn't be trusted not to touch her, then it was all the more likely that he couldn't be trusted in other ways. Why *had* he sent for her? Why his sudden interest ten years too late—when she was grown? Had he actually thought that she would fall into his arms out of gratitude? Hadn't it been enough that he had taken advantage of her father? Did he want to take advantage of her, too? Had he imagined that he would dazzle her with dollars?

Well, she decided wearily, she wouldn't find out anything by lying in bed. And he had said that he wanted to talk to her. By the time she coaxed herself into the bathroom to comb her hair she realized that the morning was already well under way. Concerned that she had slept late and not wanting to impose on Letti, she pulled on her robe and hurried down the long hallway and many stairs to the kitchen. She found Letti wiping off a big stove, but she didn't see Damon anywhere.

"Am I late to breakfast?" she asked, uneasily aware that it seemed to be over.

"You're not late to breakfast, honey," Letti assured her. "You can have breakfast anytime. It's only the evening meal that Damon sets rules for."

"Is the master coming to breakfast?" Alex asked, unable to resist the gibe.

"Damon? Oh, no. Damon ate at six a.m. and he's already gone."

"Gone?" Alex repeated. "Will he be back for dinner?"

"No, not tonight. He has business out of state. He won't be back for two weeks."

"Two weeks?" Alex felt suddenly strange on hearing the information. She greeted her host's departure with an inexplicable mixture of relief and bewilderment. Why hadn't Damon told her that last night would be his only chance to talk with her? He could have said that he wouldn't be home when she awakened. She actually did want to discuss her plans with him, and she would have talked with him last night if he had mentioned that he wouldn't be home for two weeks. Was the talk the only reason he had come to her room? Had she wrongly accused him? No, she decided. A man who looked at her the way he did had more on his mind than *her* future plans!

Running a hand through her hair, Alex went to the dining room table and sat down while Letti cooked bacon and eggs for her. She wasn't used to being waited on and she didn't like the feeling. She was an excellent cook and for some time she had been in the position of cooking for her mother and herself. Restless, she rose from the table and looked around the dining room before returning to the kitchen, where Letti was just slipping two sunny-side-up eggs on a bright blue willow-patterned plate. Sitting down at the table across from the stove, Alex watched as Letti placed two slices of bacon and two honey-brown biscuits beside the eggs. "Do you want grits?"

"Grits?" Alex repeated, unable to suppress a slight laugh. "They sound awful. What are they?"

Amusement showed in Letti's dark eyes. "Hominy—boiled corn. Most Southerners love them."

"None for me, thank you," Alex said, shaking her head. "I don't even care for the sound of them. But will you teach me to make that persimmon pudding you served last night? It was delicious."

"I'd be real happy to teach you," Letti said, beaming. The compliment obviously pleased her.

"May I eat in here, Letti?"

"Sure you can, if you want to. You can do as you please in this house—" She paused to look at Alex. With a twinkle in her eyes, she completed the sentence: "—as long as Damon doesn't mind."

"I see." Letti's statement confirmed her preconceptions of Damon as self-centered, arrogant, and domineering. And she had no idea how many less complimentary terms would fit the man. She wondered if Letti knew what plans Damon had for her. How much of a confidante was Letti to him? Obviously Letti knew about the rift between Damon and her father. Alex decided to take a chance and ask for more information. "Tell me about him, Letti. Why did he want me to come here to live?"

Letti settled down into a chair and smiled at Alex. "Because he's a good man. And I ought to know; I just about raised that boy. When he was young, I went to work for his mama and daddy as a housekeeper. They were just getting started in their clothing business then—Damon's mama even did all the alterations—and they were as busy as farmers at harvest time. Damon was an only child and it kind of got to be him and me mostly. His parents loved him, but he was my boy," she boasted fondly. "Still is."

Alex wondered just what Letti would think of her "boy" if she knew how he had behaved last night. It was plain that the old woman adored him, and Alex didn't have the heart to enlighten her about her "good" man. "Why isn't he married?" Alex sliced a biscuit and laid the two pieces of bacon on the steaming white inside. She had a good idea why, but she was discreet enough to keep it to herself.

Letti laughed somewhere deep inside, causing her plump middle to jiggle. "Doesn't seem to be a woman who can tame that boy," she said, as if it were a thing to take pride in. "It'll take more woman than any he's met up with to harness him."

Alex could believe that, and he'd be darn lucky, she thought, if he ever found one insensitive enough to endure him and his insolent ways. Since Letti seemed amicable and willing to talk, Alex edged closer to the subject she really wanted answers on. "Where are his secretarial schools?"

"He's got one here in Danville, one in Florida, one in Georgia, and he's building one in New York. He's done right well for himself. He's quite the businessman, quite well known, and folks respect him. I'm proud of him. His schools turn out some of the best secretaries in the country, so people say. I suspect you'll be enrolled in one yourself when the new classes begin. Damon wants you to get settled in and learn your way around first."

"I will not be enrolled in his school," Alex blurted, shocked by the information. "I don't intend to become a secretary. I'm going to become a veterinarian." Just who does he think he is? she fumed. First he insulted her. Then he invaded her room. And now he planned her future for her without even consulting her. The man's gall was incredible. Did he think because she had

agreed to her mother's request that she was incapable
of choosing a career?

"A veterinarian? You mean you want to doctor
animals? Why, isn't that a peculiar job for a young
lady?"

"Oh, not anymore, Letti. Women have all kinds of
careers these days. There are lots of female veterinarians, and I've always wanted to work with animals."

"But, Alex, what do you know about animal doctor-
ing?"

"Not much yet." Alex smiled. "But I'm going to
learn. I want to work with small animals—companion
animals. I hope I can get a job with the animal shelter
here. It will help with my career."

Letti's dark brows met in a frown. "Oh, Damon
won't want you to work while you're here. Anyway,
you won't need to. He'll give you an allowance."

"Well, I won't take it!" Alex stated, wondering
under just what pretense and with what expectation the
man intended to give her money. She didn't care what
he wanted. "I mean to make my own way. I won't take
his money; it's enough that he's providing me with
room and board." And I'm not so sure about that, she
wanted to add.

Letti grimly shook her head. "Heaven help us," she
muttered, "my Indian blood tells me there's going to be
war in this house when Damon comes home. He's not a
man to be swayed in his determinations."

And neither am I, Alex thought defiantly, realizing
as she looked at the older woman that she hadn't
learned anything about the feud between her father and
Damon. Well, she wouldn't let Damon manipulate her,
and she was determined to find out how he had
wronged her father. She stared at Letti for a few
seconds, trying to decide how to approach the topic of
the secretarial schools again. Taking the bull by the
horns, she asked, "Letti, what happened between
Damon and my father?"

Letti's face became a remote mask in seconds. She looked down at her large hands. "Didn't your parents ever tell you?"

"No. I only knew that my father was so angry with Damon over something he had done that his name was forbidden in our house. And I also knew that the secretarial schools Damon made his money on started with my father's idea."

Letti's gaze shot to Alex's face. Her eyes were full of emotion, but Alex couldn't decide what kind. Was it fear? Was it shame? "Honey, it's said and done now. I think it's best forgotten. It's all water under the bridge."

"Letti, please," Alex coaxed, unwilling to let the chance slip by. "I need to know."

A deep sigh caused Letti's shoulders to rise and fall as she studied the girl. "Oh, Alex, I don't see that it'll do any good, you knowing, since you don't already know."

Alex laid down her fork and reached across to take Letti's hand. She was surprised to see Letti's eyes become misty. "Please tell me, Letti. It's important to me." Her eyes were pleading. She was sure she was about to learn the truth at last.

Letti's eyes lowered. "Oh, honey, I'm not sure anyone knows what really happened. Times were bad. The business was about to fold, and to make things worse your father thought your mother—oh, don't ask me, Alex," she said, shaking her head. "You ask Damon. I don't know the real story, and I'm not a woman to judge." She got up from her chair and took the pans from the stove to the dishwasher.

"Letti—" Alex sighed. She had failed again. Letti pretended to be totally involved in her work, and Alex was left to stare at the remains of her breakfast. She was more confused than ever. Had her mother been involved in the trouble? It was apparent that Letti would say no more but that, whatever had happened, it bothered the woman.

Realizing that it was futile to question Letti any further now and wanting to lighten the heavy atmosphere, Alex forced herself to ask cheerfully, "What are the plans for the day, Letti? I'd like to see the town. Do you think we could do that today?"

Happy with the change in subject, Letti turned to Alex. "My, but you're in a hurry. If you want, I can show you the town today. The house cleaner arrives at nine and we'll go then. But first, don't you want to see the rest of the house? You hardly had time to see the dining room and your room last night."

Alex smiled. "I'd love to." She had wondered if she would be permitted to see the rooms in which the imposing, tyrannical Mr. Montaigne lived, but she didn't want to seem audacious by tramping over the house unescorted on her first day there. Trying to put thoughts of her father out of her mind, she followed Letti to the living room.

Gorgeous, with dark wood-paneled walls, the room had a massive red-brick fireplace adorned with antique andirons and an intricate firescreen. The colonial furniture, a brightly patterned settee and colorful armchairs of several solid shades, grouped with fancy long-legged tables, was embellished with the lush greenery of numerous potted plants. A beautiful grandfather clock announced the time with deep-toned chimes.

Alex followed as Letti led her through the various rooms. When they entered the library, Alex was overwhelmed by the towering floor-to-ceiling shelves, filled with books of every description. "Oh, do you think I could take some books from here to read?" she asked, impressed with Damon's collection.

"Of course. Suit yourself. But whatever you do, don't touch Damon's chess pieces." Letti gestured to the many chess sets sitting about the room. "They're his pride and joy." On one slim table sat a lavish ebony-and-ivory-checkered board with delicate clear-glass pieces. Carved green figures, apparently jade, sat on a hand-tooled leather board on another table. All around the room were the most beautiful and the most ornate chess sets Alex had ever imagined.

"Damon is a real good player," Letti commented. "Do you play?"

Alex laughed lightly. "No, I'm afraid not. I hardly know the pieces. I think I lack the concentration necessary to learn the game. I'm much too impatient to figure out the strategy."

"I don't play either," Letti admitted, "but, I can tell you, Damon is real crazy about the game. He looks at everyone as a possible partner."

"He won't find one in me," Alex assured her. Even if she knew the game, she would never play with him.

Alex was surprised by the homey atmosphere of Damon's rooms; she had expected his living quarters to be as harsh and overbearing as she found him to be. However, the rooms were warmly done in browns and greens. There appeared to be a small office set in an alcove and a chess set was on the large desk. Just as they started to leave the room, Alex noticed the tall file cabinet sitting in the corner of the alcove. Even from where she stood she could read the drawer labels, and she knew that the secretarial school records were kept there. Her heartbeats increased. Would Damon have records going back as far as ten years? Would it be worth taking a chance to find information about the school her father and he had started? Surely if he had cheated her father, it wouldn't be down in black and white. On the other hand, maybe she could learn something that would prove useful.

"Alex?" Letti questioned. "Coming?"

Alex laughed lightly. "Yes. Yes, of course. I don't know what I was thinking of." She quickly followed

Letti from the room, but her thoughts were whirling. The first chance she had, she would examine the files.

When Letti had shown Alex all of the house, she went back downstairs. Alex went to her rooms and slipped into a white shirt with tiny green flowers and darker green slacks; she wondered if she should top the outfit with a sweater as well as her blue jacket. She had forgotten how cold the January air could be. She seemed to have forgotten everything about the town she had spent her younger years in. It seemed that, like her mother and father, she had left all thoughts of it behind when she went to California. Looking out the window in an attempt to guess the temperature, she was surprised to see that the night had left a frost on the ground. The grass, coated with white, looked as if it would crunch beneath her feet; Alex shivered as she looked at the patchy green-brown color. But the grounds were still gorgeous. Numerous trees were in various stages of defoliation. Some stretched bare arms to a moody gray sky; others obstinately flaunted green leaves in defiance of winter's cold cape. Seized with a sudden impulse to partake of the beauty of the Virginia hills firsthand, Alex pulled on her blue jacket, slid her feet into her brown loafers, and hurried down the hallway. She passed Letti on her dash down the stairs.

"Slow down on these stairs, Alex," Letti cautioned, shaking her finger in warning.

"Oh, Letti, the grounds look so beautiful from my window. I'm going to take a look."

Letti nodded a head thickly wrapped in graying braids. "They are beautiful. But you ought to wrap up better. It's cold out this morning."

In her haste, Alex ignored the warning about the cold and charged outside. After the crowds and congestion of California, this wide-open country enchanted her. She hadn't expected such beauty in the Old South, and as she looked around a feeling of peace settled over her. She breathed deeply, feeling the cold crispness of the air as she went out on the mansion's wide porch. Two ancient weeping willow trees, with dipping branches bare of leaves, guarded Willowstone on either side, their lofty stature causing her to feel insignificant as she stepped out on the sleeping lawn. Hugging her arms to her body, she walked down the rosebush-lined walkway and looked back at the stately mansion.

It was overpowering in its handsomeness. The two-story house displayed expansive two-tiered porticos fronted by four massive white columns. Twelve wide steps led up to the huge front door, which supported a large brass knocker. The walls of the house, brick laid in flemish bond, were almost obscured by the flourishing ivy that had claimed them. The roof hosted four brick chimneys. The sheer beauty of the house took her breath away.

Setting off along the magnolia-lined driveway, Alex found that it wound around the back of the house to pass stores of corded wood stacked against a wall. A small neat cottage sat ten to fifteen yards from the main house, and Alex could see George Willis moving about behind a window. A short way from his house, she saw a shallow stream partially frozen in the coldness of the morning, a vine-covered gazebo edging close to its bank. The whinny of horses drew her attention to two red stables surrounded by white fences to the west of the main house.

She heard a car approaching and suppressed a desire to check out the stables, and instead she started back toward the mansion. A Cadillac, long, sleek, and golden, had stopped under the magnolia trees.

When Alex approached, a lovely woman opened the car door and swung beautiful long legs to the pavement. Stepping from the car, she called to Alex. "Well, hello there, and who might you be?"

Her voice was very feminine, almost purring in its smoothness. Her smile was full and radiant, showing perfect teeth in a startling white complexion. Masses of black curls tumbled down the woman's back, and her large violet eyes, fringed by sweeping, sooty lashes, questioned Alex.

"I'm Alex Hawthorne." Alex felt small and plain in the shadow of the woman's elegance. As she looked at the woman, she was reminded of the beautiful, sheltered Southern belles she had read about, and she had the feeling that, like the belles in the books, this one would present only the face she wanted the viewer to see.

A finely arched eyebrow shot up as the violet eyes raked over Alex. "Oh, you're Damon's orphan, Lena Hawthorne's daughter. How could I have missed the resemblance? I didn't really expect you to come. And Damon certainly didn't tell me you had arrived."

Was it Alex's imagination, or were the woman's words bitter—even vicious?

Alex tried to hide the irritation she felt at being called Damon's orphan. "I only arrived last night."

"Regardless, Damon should have phoned me." The red lips pouted. There was something in the woman's manner that more than subtly stated that Damon was intimately connected with her—and that Alex's appearance wasn't pleasing to her. Alex tried to tell herself that she was imagining things—but was she?

"I'm Casaundra Calahan," the woman said. It definitely wasn't Alex's imagination that the woman paused, searching her face carefully—almost as if she expected Alex to recognize the name. Alex was very uncomfortable under the hard look, and she was glad when Casaundra extended a long, slim, beautiful hand tipped by brightly painted nails. She was charmingly wrapped up against the January cold in a cashmere sweater, brown wool skirt with a fashionable side slit, and ankle-high boots of brown leather. A shimmering lilac blouse gave her violet eyes a stunning cast. A three-quarter-length fur coat was slung carelessly over her shoulders.

Alex, taking her hand lightly, found it to be very cold.

"You really don't know who I am, do you?" Casaundra asked.

Alex shook her head.

Casaundra's eyes shifted as she carefully measured Alex. "I'm Damon's . . . friend." She stared into Alex's eyes for a moment. "I think you and I need to get acquainted. Come on. Let's go inside and get Letti to make us some coffee."

Her curiosity heightened, Alex followed the older woman into the house. She was mildly surprised by Casaundra's proprietary manner. She moved down the hallway calling, "Letti! Letti, where are you?"

Almost immediately, Letti appeared at the top of the stairs. "Yes, Miss Calahan?" Alex was surprised at the formality that had replaced Letti's usually friendly manner.

"Did Damon get off all right this morning?"

"Yes, Miss Calahan."

"Bring some coffee to the living room," Casaundra ordered. "And Damon was to have left some financial reports for me. Bring those, too."

Her normally smiling black eyes totally devoid of any emotion, Letti nodded. "Yes, Miss Calahan. Please make yourself comfortable. I'll be there in a few minutes." Her dull eyes met Alex's briefly before she started dutifully down the stairs.

Casaundra touched a hand to Alex's elbow to prompt her toward the living room. Glimpsing her reflection in the large mantel mirror, she patted a stray black curl before she settled herself on the patterned settee. She crossed her shapely legs and stared at Alex as Alex sat in the armchair across from her.

"Now tell me"—Casaundra's eyes glowed with interest—"what's our Damon going to do with you? He's hardly used to having a—a girl in the house. It was unfortunate that you were orphaned, but still, I never

expected you here in Willowstone. Not after your
father—I mean after what happened—" Her words
trailed off and she looked down to study her nails.

There it was again—that implication that her father
was somehow to blame for the feud instead of Damon
Montaigne. "Just what *did* happen?" Alex insisted.

A strange smile touched Casaundra's lips. "You
don't know?"

"No, I don't know," Alex confessed, "and no one
seems to want to tell me."

Casaundra shrugged her shoulders and widened her
eyes. "Well, my dear Alex, far be it from me to air such
dirty—to talk about it with you. Well, I just—why, I
assumed you knew."

"Knew what?" Alex persisted.

A polite smile turned up the corner of Casaundra's
lips. "I'm sure that will have to be between Damon and
you, Alex. I'm just curious as to what on earth the man
is going to do with you."

"Damon isn't going to *do* anything with me. I'm
quite capable of running my own life. I'll either work or
go to school; I'm not sure which. I haven't had time to
discuss the matter with Damon." Alex shifted uneasily
in the chair. Under Casaundra's scrutiny and because
of the other woman's knowledge of the breakup
between Damon and Alex's father, Alex felt defensive.
It did seem odd that she was staying with Damon—
even to her. "I'm only here because I made a promise
to my mother. She was very ill, you see, and I couldn't
refuse her request."

Alex was sure a wicked gleam came into Casaundra's
eyes. "Oh, I see, I see. Of course, your mother would
have a hand in it, wouldn't she?" Her eyes became
thoughtful, and Alex wondered what she meant. It was
several minutes before she spoke again. "If you do
attend school, you'll go to Damon's secretarial school
here, won't you? I manage that school. Not that I need
to work, you understand. The Calahans are very old

money, as they say, but working keeps me . . . in touch, if you know what I mean."

Alex was certain she had received more information than she needed, but she wasn't really interested in Casaundra's innuendos. Apparently the woman was trying to protect her interests in Damon, whatever they might be. Well, if she wanted the man, she was welcome to him. But, Alex mused uneasily, if Casaundra was worried about her being under the same roof with Damon, perhaps *she* had reason to worry, too. Casaundra most certainly knew him better than she did, though why any woman should want him was a puzzle. He was thoroughly disagreeable. Alex was also annoyed that it seemed to be an accepted fact that she would attend his secretarial school when she hadn't even been consulted. She was being treated as though she had no say in her own future. Damon's nerve was unbelievable! "Actually, Miss Calahan—"

"Oh, my dear, do call me Casaundra. After all, I did know your parents."

"You knew my parents?" Alex repeated. "Were you a friend of theirs?"

Casaundra smiled. "An acquaintance." It was apparent that she was going to say nothing else.

Alex tried to think of a tactful way to elicit more information from the woman, but, frustrated, she knew that once again she would have to bide her time. "Well, anyway . . . Casaundra . . . I won't be going to Damon's school."

"No?" The purr of her voice became more pronounced. "Why, I'm sure Damon thought—well, never mind what Damon thought." She gave a throaty laugh. "Just what *are* your plans?"

Alex's first impulse was to ask what business it was of hers, but she decided not to antagonize the woman. She still might be able to learn something from her about her father and Damon's relationship. And Casaundra did seem actually interested in her plans. "I want to become a veterinarian."

"A veterinarian! Working with dirty, diseased animals? Really, Alex, wherever did you get such a preposterous idea?" Amusement twinkled in Casaundra's violet eyes.

Alex tried to control her rising anger. "It's not preposterous!" she insisted defensively. "It's a fine profession. There are different kinds of veterinarians, you know!"

"No, I wasn't in the know on that little tidbit of information," Casaundra remarked dryly, obviously bored by Alex's outburst. "But I do know something about the profession. I have a friend who's a vet, and I was surprised to find that it's no simple undertaking. You must be aware that it's quite expensive to attend veterinary school, and that it requires years of study."

"I—yes," Alex murmured uncertainly. Truthfully, she wasn't sure of the cost or the length of study since she had only made up her mind to become a veterinarian at the end of her first college semester. When her mother's illness had intensified, she hadn't been able to devote any time to her uncertain future. It had been a struggle just to get through each day. She felt her cheeks grow pink; she was embarrassed by her lack of knowledge and ashamed that she had spouted off about something she obviously lacked information on.

"How interesting." Casaundra toyed with a large emerald dinner ring on her finger. "A female veterinarian." The idea seemed to intrigue her. "And what about your immediate plans? Will you be going away to school soon?"

Alex thought she sounded hopeful. She had the feeling that the woman didn't care for her continued presence. "Going away?" She hadn't considered going away to school but that wasn't in her immediate plans anyway. She wanted to stay and find out more about

her father and Damon Montaigne. "No, I'll get settled
in here until the fall semester of school. The interim
period will give me time to decide on my plans and
make adequate arrangements. I haven't even seen the
town, and I want to try to get a job at the local animal
shelter."

"You mean the pound?" Casaundra's eyes widened
in surprise. "Working with those wretched cast-off cats
and dogs?"

"Yes," Alex said succinctly. She was already quite
sure that she and Casaundra weren't going to be any
better friends than she and Damon. Both of them had
managed to anger her during their first encounter.

Casaundra seemed to smirk and a gleam appeared in
her eyes. "I'll show you the town and take you to the
pound," she suddenly announced, almost too eagerly.
"Get your wrap and let's go."

Startled by her decisiveness and annoyed that she
hadn't asked if Alex wanted to go with her, Alex said,
"But Letti and I have already made plans to see the
town today. And, besides, she's making coffee for us.
Remember?"

The protests were dismissed with a wave of Casaundra's elegant hand. "Oh, for heaven's sake, that
doesn't matter. She should have been more prompt.
Come on. Let's go."

"I must explain to Letti," Alex countered determinedly as she hurried from the room. When she
reached the kitchen, Letti was just pouring two cups of
coffee from a sterling silver coffeepot. Watching her set
the pot on the tray, Alex murmured, "It seems that we
won't be needing the coffee now, Letti. Casaundra is
ready to leave. As a matter of fact, she insists on
showing me the town herself." Embarrassment clouded
Alex's eyes. She liked Letti, and she didn't want to
damage her relationship with her. "I told her we had
other plans, Letti, but she just wouldn't listen."

"Oh, that woman," Letti muttered, dark eyes narrowed with displeasure.

Casaundra materialized behind them as if by magic. "You heard her, Letti. I'll show her the town. I'm sure you're much too busy to chauffeur Damon's guests around. I'll take her to the pound."

"Now you wait just a minute, Miss Calahan. I don't think Alex needs to see the pound. Damon hasn't discussed—"

"That's always been a problem of yours, Letti," Casaundra interrupted coldly. "You've never known your place. Don't you tell me what to do!" Ignoring Letti's angry snort, she picked up a manila folder that was lying by the coffee tray. "I'm ready, Alex."

Alex wasn't sure what to do now that she was caught up in the verbal battle between the women. "Shall I go, Letti?" she asked, not wanting to annoy Casaundra further, but not wanting to rudely leave Letti after they had made plans.

"For crying out loud, Alex," Casaundra snapped, "you don't need a servant's permission to go!"

"Miss Calahan"—Letti's voice was hard—"some people aren't as rude as you are. Alex and I had made plans." She turned to Alex and gave her a motherly pat. "You go ahead and enjoy yourself, honey."

A flame danced in Casaundra's eyes as she turned and sauntered out of the kitchen.

Flinging an apologetic look at Letti, Alex followed uncertainly. She couldn't imagine Damon permitting anyone to speak to Letti in such a condescending manner. She could tell that Damon was fond of Letti, and she was shocked by Casaundra's blatant disregard for the other woman's feelings. However, Alex could definitely see Casaundra as Damon's friend; they seemed suited. For some vague reason, the thought unsettled her.

Chapter Three

The old city, nestled under massing clouds in a gray-tinged sky, proved to be quite fascinating. A hilly mixture of very new and very old construction, it was situated around the muddy Dan River, which separated the two main hills. At the end of the old cement bridge crossing the turbulent waters, Casaundra and Alex drove past an ancient, red-brick building with dark windows. "The cotton mill," Casaundra pointed out blandly as Alex stared at the building. "The Dan River Mills comprise the largest single-unit textile mill in the world and were first established in eighteen eighty-two by six Danvillians. I have to know such information for the students coming into the city for school."

"I've seen bed linen with the Dan River label," Alex remarked, "but I never knew it came from here. I had no idea that the town contained so much history. In fact, I hated the idea of coming back here, but it may prove fascinating."

Casaundra cocked an eyebrow in Alex's direction, "Yes, it may," she mused pensively. "It very well may. For all of us."

Alex tried to ignore the insinuation in the statement. She wanted to like Casaundra, despite the rocky start to their relationship, but a sixth sense warned her that the older woman couldn't be trusted. There was some mystery about her parents' relationship with Damon Montaigne and it seemed that a lot of people knew something about it, but no one was willing to tell her. She was determined to find some answers somewhere, but she didn't think they would come from Casaundra. Deliberately skirting Casaundra's remark, Alex asked, "Are there good schools here?"

"Yes, there are."

"I'm glad to hear that. My education is very important to me."

Casaundra's laugh was throaty. "My dear Alex, I'm glad to hear that."

When it seemed that Casaundra was heading back toward Willowstone, Alex asked, "Aren't we going to the pound? I realize that Letti didn't think much of the idea before it was discussed with Damon, but . . ."

"No?" Casaundra questioned. "Well, you're a big girl now, aren't you? You don't need Damon's consent. We're on our way to the pound."

"I know I don't need Damon's consent," Alex agreed, "but I am living in his house and naturally I don't want to offend him any more than I can help." She didn't want to add that she and Damon had already gotten off to a bad start and that she was sure it was going to be difficult enough living with him without deliberately antagonizing him.

"No, of course not," Casaundra agreed, but the broad smile she gave Alex was a decidedly mischievous one. It made Alex wonder once again about the underlying motive for her interest and the veiled hostility behind her insinuations. Did Casaundra know something about Damon that Alex should know, or was she just plain jealous?

Alex's concern about offending Damon by getting a job was unnecessary. When she and Casaundra inquired, they found that the shelter was fully staffed and was taking only volunteer workers. Even Casaundra's haughty insistence that Alex could surely be worked in a few days a week received a negative reply.

They had just left the office and were walking down the corridor when a slender, golden-blond man of medium height approached them, carrying a kitten in a cage. Nicely dressed in a tailored jump suit of light green, he was so preoccupied with the kitten that he didn't seem to notice them.

"Well, if it isn't Brent Haggerman! What are you doing here?" Casaundra exclaimed.

"Casaundra! How are you?" he asked, looking up. "And what brings you here is the question. You don't usually show up in these parts."

Moving toward him possessively, Casaundra offered him her cheek. He gave her a light peck and smiled, causing his pleasant, almost serene face to come alive and his blue eyes to sparkle. "And who's this little beauty?" He surveyed Alex boldly.

"Well, well, Brent," Casaundra said, "you obviously like what you see. This little beauty, to quote you, is Alex Hawthorne—Lena's child—and Damon's little orphan." She let the spaced words drop distinctly from her lips.

Alex didn't miss the flash of surprise that lit up Brent's eyes. Looking from the woman to the girl, he held out his hand to Alex. "So you're Damon's guest. I heard you might be coming, but I didn't expect such a pretty little thing. I'm Brent Haggerman, the local vet. I'm very pleased to meet you. Casaundra, Damon, and I are old friends, aren't we, sweet?" he asked, turning to give Casaundra a peculiar look.

Alex was puzzled by the strained smile they exchanged. Brent had seemed to be less comfortable after Casaundra told him she was Damon's orphan and she didn't know what to think about it.

"How do you do?" Alex asked politely, taking in his bright eyes, curly blond hair, and wide mouth above a chiseled jawline. A slender man who was probably a couple of years younger than Damon, he was handsome in a sensitive way, but it was his profession, not his looks, that captured Alex's attention.

"Alex wanted to work here at the pound," Casaundra explained, "but there were no openings."

Brent looked surprised. "You wanted to work here, Miss Hawthorne?"

"Please call me Alex," she said. "And yes, I did want to work here. I want to become a veterinarian."

"Please call me Brent." He grinned boyishly at her. "A vet—indeed?" He rubbed his angular chin thoughtfully. "I wonder, Alex," he mused. "Does Damon know what he's taken on with you?"

Casaundra, smiling broadly, reached out to touch Brent's hand familiarly. "I hardly think so."

Alex's attention was attracted to the yowling kitten in the cage. "He's a noisy one," she commented, grateful for the distraction.

Brent opened the cage door and removed a small, long-haired, smoke-colored animal. The kitten's face was sad and one ear drooped forlornly, making him look slightly ridiculous. "I found him abandoned by the side of the road, apparently thrown from a moving vehicle. I sewed him up, but I don't have much hope that he'll find a home." Turning the kitten's head so that Alex could see where he had been treated, Brent said, "I'm afraid his ear is irreparably damaged. He'll probably end up on death row."

Alex's eyes were instantly pained. "Oh, but he's so beautiful."

"Beautiful? Hardly. And cats are a dime a dozen."

"I know," Alex murmured sadly. "I worked in a shelter in California, and I was appalled at the number of animals destroyed because of lack of homes." Hit with a sudden weakness for the animal, she turned to Casaundra. "You know Damon better than I do. Do you think he would object if I took the kitten to Willowstone?"

Casaundra and Brent exchanged a knowing glance. "I'm afraid Damon isn't much of an animal person, except with his horses," Brent explained.

"Oh, what can one little cat hurt?" Casaundra asked, her voice honey sweet.

Alex didn't miss the curious glance Brent cast in her direction. "You know what one little cat could hurt. Damon could throw a fit about it. I *do* think he will object and I *don't* want to be a party to anything Damon Montaigne objects to. After all, whatever Damon wants, Damon gets."

Alex thought the statement sounded almost belligerent, but as she looked at his face, she wondered if she had been mistaken.

"For heaven's sake, Brent," Casaundra snapped, "give her the cat. She wants it. Damon's away on business and the thing will be put to sleep before he returns. Besides," she added with a slight smile, "no daughter of Lena Hawthorne's would be intimidated by Damon's temper."

"As you wish, Casaundra," Brent demurred in his mellow voice, "as you wish; but I hope you're willing to stand accountable when the devil claims his due."

Alex was aware of a half-concealed venom in his tone that she thought inappropriate to the situation, and she was sure there was some underlying meaning to Casaundra's statement. She watched as Brent and Casaundra's eyes locked momentarily, and she had the feeling that theirs was an old battle.

"I'm certainly not afraid of Damon's temper," Alex said smoothly, holding out her hand for the kitten. She didn't know what had gotten into her, but some perverse impulse made her want to challenge Damon. So he always got what he wanted, did he? Surely it was time that changed.

Taking the kitten from Brent, she held it against her body. She decided to leave the two friends to their own ends. "It was nice to meet you, Brent. I'll wait for you by the car, Casaundra."

"The pleasure is all mine, Alex," Brent said. His blue eyes sparkled again as they traveled easily over her. "I hope to see a lot more of you."

Alex was down the hall and out of hearing distance when she remembered that she hadn't thanked Brent for the kitten. As she walked back down the hall to where he and Casaundra stood with their backs to her, she heard Brent say, "Surely not that young woman, Casaundra. Don't try any of your tricks. I mean it; I won't stand by and see it happen again."

Alex's heartbeats picked up. Surely he couldn't be talking about her, could he? His voice had sounded so—so threatening. What tricks had Casaundra been up to? Alex shook her head to clear it. Of course, he wasn't making reference to her. Casaundra didn't even know her. "Excuse me," she said quickly. "I forgot to thank you for the cat."

Obviously startled, both of them turned toward her. Casaundra's eyes were hard, and it took Brent a moment to manage a smile. "You're certainly welcome."

Nodding, Alex walked back down the hall. Casaundra caught up with her at the front of the building. "What'll you name the cat?" she asked sweetly, all traces of her former hostility gone.

Alex nuzzled the little bundle of fur that trembled slightly. "Oh, I think I'll call him Roadside, because that's where he was found."

The moody gray skies of morning had begun to darken considerably. Suddenly, they opened up to deluge the women with rain as they approached the car. Struggling with the door handles, Casaundra and Alex hurried inside, but not before they were hit by the

pelting drops. During the return trip to Willowstone,
with only a quick stop to pick up supplies for Roadside,
the car was curiously silent.

"I won't come in," Casaundra said when she drove
up the driveway. "Enjoy the cat." She smiled mockingly, causing Alex to wonder what she was up to.

"Thanks." Stuffing Roadside in her jacket front and
grabbing her bags, she stepped out of the car and
rushed to the porch. She was glad that she had rescued
the little kitten, and now that she was back at the
mansion, she was determined to think of some way to
keep the animal.

When she opened the door of the house, she smelled
the sweet aroma of pipe tobacco. Immediately, she
thought of Damon, but she knew he was in New York.
She wondered if there were guests in the house. She
hoped they wouldn't see her; she was quite a sight with
her wet clothing and damp hair, and she had wanted to
show Roadside to Letti before anyone else saw him.
Back in Damon's domain, she already felt less certain
about her impulse to adopt the kitten.

Avoiding the living room, she left her bags in the
kitchen and searched the house for Letti, but the
woman wasn't to be found. Alex was left with no choice
but to find out who was in the living room. She waited
outside the door for a few seconds, listening for voices,
but she heard none. Thinking the room must be empty,
regardless of the smell of smoke, she opened the door
and stepped inside.

She saw Damon sitting in a beige wingback chair
before the fireplace; her hand froze on the doorknob,
and she gasped ever so slightly. Damon was holding his
hands out before the fire. His soaked black shoes were
by his chair, and he had raised his gray-socked feet
toward the fire's heat. He drew deeply on his pipe and
exhaled slowly. Despite the homey scene, Alex thought
he looked even more formidable than usual. Watching

him warily as he settled wearily back into the soft chair and closed his eyes, she started to slip from the room.

The movement made her lose her grip on Roadside. Before she could grab him, he crouched low and began to sneak to the back of Damon's chair to investigate the stranger. Walking on tiptoe behind him, hoping against hope that she wouldn't disturb Damon before she could apprehend the elusive kitten, Alex pursued.

Damon opened one eye and cocked an eyebrow warily as she neared his chair. His voice was deep and tired. "Would you mind telling me what you're doing?"

The sudden sound of his voice startled Roadside into action. Faster than any recently injured kitten should have been able to do, he tore up the back of the chair, rushed over the top, down across a thoroughly surprised Damon, and out the door.

Alex backed away as Damon jumped up and glared at her. When she saw his expression, she was tempted to flee behind the terrified Roadside.

"What the devil!" Damon exclaimed. "What's going on here? What's the meaning of this, Alex? Can't a man even relax in his own living room?"

Alex's breathing quickened. Damon was standing very close to her, but today she had no worries that he might try to force himself on her. There was none of the passion in his eyes that she had glimpsed so briefly during their last meeting. Standing there before him now, she was certain that she'd misjudged his motives for coming to her room. He seemed actually to hate her as his eyes bore down into hers.

"Well?" he demanded.

She tossed back her blond hair and tried to meet his hard eyes, but her heart was fluttering so wildly that she couldn't keep up the pretense of calm. "I—I'm sorry, Damon," she stammered, feeling ridiculous. When she had said she wasn't afraid of Damon's temper, she certainly hadn't counted on seeing so much of it.

She looked about the room nervously before forcing herself to display some measure of composure. Damon's eyes were smoldering with anger and hers were still saucer size with alarm as she tried to explain. "That was—it is—I got a kitten today. I hope you don't mind."

Damon continued to stare at her incredulously without speaking. She was compelled by the look in his eyes to offer further explanation. "You see, he didn't have a home, and, well," she added with sudden defiance, trying to gain some control of the situation, "Letti did say you wanted me to make myself at home."

An ominous crashing noise from the library made Alex stop speaking abruptly. For just a moment she was rooted to the spot where she stood as she considered the terrible possibility of what had probably happened. Finally forcing herself into movement, she fled in the direction of the noise. Through the open door, Roadside stared at her with wild green eyes as he gingerly picked his way through the broken pieces of Damon's glass chessmen.

Alex's heart sank. She could sense Damon's presence behind her, but she didn't dare turn around. Scooping up Roadside with one hand before he could cause more damage, she bent down to pick up the thin, fragile pieces of the chessmen that seemed to have shattered into a thousand slivers.

The voice behind her was stern. "Hand-blown glass from Italy, Miss Hawthorne. I've had that set for eight years without a piece being so much as chipped."

Reluctantly, Alex turned to face the tall man who, from her position on the floor, looked even taller than he actually was. His eyes flicked over her. She was sure he despised her. "I'm terribly sorry, Damon. Please believe me. I'll have the broken ones replaced," she sputtered quickly. Her dignity was as shattered as the glass chessmen, and she was mortified that she had been responsible for so much damage in so short a time.

"I'm happy to hear that, Miss Hawthorne. The set cost two thousand dollars," Damon stated flatly.

Alex's heart jumped. "It may take me a while, but I *will* replace them," she insisted foolishly.

She turned back to her futile chore, which was only complicated by the struggling Roadside. When she looked around for somewhere to deposit the pieces, Damon was gone. She felt tears come to her eyes, but she resisted the temptation to weep. She should never have promised her mother that she would come here; if her mother had remembered Damon at all, she should have realized the situation would be impossible. The man was absolutely frightening. She let the pieces of shimmering glass drop from her hand and sat down on the cool wood floor. "Oh, Roadside," she whispered, "you've gotten me into a lot of trouble." It had been foolhardy to bring the kitten to Willowstone; both of them might be looking for a new home in a short time.

Arching his smoky back, Roadside walked possessively over Alex's lap, purring contentedly. A gasp from the doorway caught Alex by surprise and she jumped.

"Heaven help us," Letti exclaimed, hurrying into the room. "What on earth happened? And where did that kitten come from?" She bent down beside Alex and touched the part of the glass queen that remained intact.

Words tumbled from Alex's trembling lips as she explained what had happened. Then she pressed her lips together and breathed deeply, trying to stem the building tears, but the sight of Letti's sympathetic face was too much. As the tears slipped down her cheeks, Letti patted her gently on the back.

"I stepped out back a minute to take George something to eat. Mostly he does his own cooking, but I like to give him a good meal once in a while. That's why you couldn't find me. And Damon's here because the worst snowstorm of the season fell on New York, so he had to put off his trip. Then he was caught in our rainstorm with a flat tire, so he's had a real bad day. But don't you worry about the chess set now. It's too late for worrying, and Damon can order another one. You stop your crying and let me get this mess cleaned up."

Still clutching Roadside, Alex struggled up from the floor. "Letti, do you think I should take him back to the shelter? I'm afraid Damon is really angry. I had no right to bring him here."

"Now don't you worry about Damon. He'll get over it." Letti held a large hand out to the softly mewing animal and it nuzzled contentedly against her fingers. She was won over in a minute. "No, wait and see what happens. Damon will get used to the cat. Besides, it might be kind of fun to have a pet around the place. I'll get a broom to clean up, but maybe you should take the kitten to your room."

Leaning close, Alex kissed the wrinkled cheek. "Thanks, Letti." Then she hurried up the steps and deposited Roadside in her room, closing the door firmly. She certainly didn't want him to be responsible for any more damage. When she returned to the library, Letti had cleaned up the broken glass and put the board and the few remaining pieces back on the table. "We'll have to keep this door closed if you keep that kitten, child," she said. "You'd best get ready for dinner. It's almost time to eat, and Damon is already in a nasty mood." With the dustpan full of broken glass, Letti left the room.

Alex dropped down in a comfortable chair to stare dismally at the few remaining pieces. Two thousand dollars! Where on earth would she ever get that kind of money?

Damon was already seated at the dining room table

studying what appeared to be some kind of financial report when Alex entered the dining room.

"Where is your animal, Alex? Did you leave him in the library to destroy more of my property?" Damon asked. "Or is he on your person, cleverly concealed and ready for another attack on me?"

It seemed that Alex couldn't even come near him without prompting some derogatory exchange between them. He had the most exasperating way of needling her, she told herself. "The kitten is in my room. What happened was an accident," she replied stiffly, turning her eyes away from his as she pulled out a chair. "You frightened him." She had intended to tell Damon that she would take the kitten back to the shelter if he was so adverse to it, but after his snide remarks, she resolved to make him insist that she get rid of Roadside if that was what he wanted.

"Isn't it rather presumptuous of you to bring an animal into the house on your second day here? Have you no regard for the wishes of others?" His manner indicated exactly what he thought of presumptuous guests.

The nerve of him to ask her if she had no regard for the wishes of others! Who was he to speak to her like that, a man who had barged in on her in her bedroom! "The kitten had no one to care for it," she replied, bristling, and she struggled to keep a civil tongue as she seated herself as far away from him as the length of the table permitted. Thank heavens, it was a big table. "I'm not as foolish as you think."

"Oh?" Damon sounded as if he doubted the truth of her statement.

She sighed wearily. "I went to the animal shelter to get a job. The kitten's life was in danger, and it was just a coincidence that I happened to be there." She toyed with her napkin, folding it in half and straightening it out again. "I—I'm sorry if you think I acted impulsively." She had to force the words from her mouth. Why should she apologize to him? It has been his idea for her to come here. Just what did he want from her?

Damon frowned menacingly and narrowed his eyes at her. "I beg your pardon. What did you say? You went to the shelter for what purpose?"

Unable to meet his hard gaze, she lowered her eyes to stare at her napkin. "I went to the shelter to get a job."

"My foolish girl, you don't need to work." His tone was patronizing. "It was the understanding between your mother and me that you would come here to complete your education. I'll grant you an allowance. There will be no need for you to work."

She raised her eyes and glared at him. "I know my mother and you had an understanding. Do you think I would be here otherwise? I'll have you know, however, that I happen to be capable of managing my own affairs." She didn't notice that he clenched his fists and that his facial muscles tightened as if he had been slapped. She tossed her head angrily. "I am an adult, in case you haven't noticed. I can work for a living. I'll need money for college, and I'll need money for personal things. You're more than generous to share your house with me, but I will not take an allowance from you. I don't want your money!"

She could see his anger rising, but she was determined not to surrender to him. "Now just a minute! Why must you be such a little hardhead?" he demanded. "Save your independence for someone who will appreciate it. I can well afford to supply you with an allowance *and* to pay for your education and that's exactly what I intend to do."

"Well, good for you!" Alex exclaimed. "*I* intend to work!" Blue eyes dancing with anger, she clenched her teeth and clung to her determination.

At just that moment, Letti came through the door and placed a platter of crispy Southern fried chicken and a dish of candied yams on the table, but Alex's stomach was churning so violently that she didn't think she would be able to swallow a bite.

Damon threw down the report and Alex started at the fury behind the motion. From the corner of her eye, she saw Letti hurry out of the room with surprising speed. "I realize that you're still very young, Alex," Damon said with slow deliberation, "and I know that the circumstances of your life have kept you sheltered. I know that you haven't had much guidance and I understand that you're at a time in your life when you aren't sure what you want, but that's the reason I've asked you to come here. However, if you're going to block me at every turn—"

"Don't speak to me as though I were a child!" she snapped. "I *do* know what I want! Besides, you know you didn't have me come here for the reasons you're suggesting!" she flared vehemently. "You feel guilty about succeeding on my father's dream while all he got out of it was a broken heart, and you're trying to salve your conscience!" She had no more expected to say the words than Damon had expected to hear them.

His face was rigid with anger, and his voice was a low growl. "You don't know what you're talking about."

"I *do* know. I watched my father fade away. You didn't have to!" She realized that she really meant it. Why should Damon have succeeded in the schools her father started? Why should her father have died disillusioned and poor? And why had Damon sent for her? His face seemed to be very pale suddenly.

He breathed heavily for a moment, then he said, "I'll just ignore that last statement. I'm trying to give you a good start in life, and I'll thank you to remember that. You couldn't have even paid the rent on that house you were living in. You're not doing *me* the favor, little girl! It's the other way around!"

"And I'll thank you to remember that I'm only here because I promised my mother on her deathbed. I would have managed somehow. I don't need favors from you, and I don't believe for a moment that you're doing this out of the goodness of your heart!"

Damon slammed his fist down on the table. "That's enough! You're being ridiculous and you know it!" He appeared to have regained his control by allowing his anger an outlet.

Alex felt that it was his intention to intimidate her, but he only succeeded in rankling her further. She got up from the table. "I despise you!"

"Do you indeed?" Damon jerked himself upright and pushed his chair away from the table. Alex's eyes grew large as he marched over to her side of the table and leaned down threateningly close. Her heart began to hammer so loudly that she was afraid he could hear it. Never had she been so conscious of a man as she was of Damon as he looked down at her now with rage plainly visible on his face.

"What you need, little girl, is to be taken firmly in hand, and I'm just the man for the job. I insist as part of our agreement that you do not work until you're settled in. If you want to damage your studies by taking on unnecessary work when you're enrolled in the business school, I'll see that you get a job there part time, but the animal shelter is out!" Alex could swear that she saw sparks ignite in the dangerous depths of his eyes.

"I'm not going to your business school," she countered icily, enjoying each word. She turned from her chair and started to leave the room. "You and I don't have any agreement. And I'm not hungry!"

Before she could take two steps, a big hand lashed out to grab her wrist. "Come back here! I've had a bad day, and I'm in no mood to indulge childish tempers! I don't care whether you're hungry or not, but you *will* remain at the table through dinner as I have previously requested, and you *will* discuss your career with me—now!"

His encircling hand bit into her flesh, and even as she stood there hating the man, trying to free herself, she felt a shock of excitement course its way up her arm as his skin seared hers. She was stunned by the sensation. She certainly wasn't attracted to this brute of a man. Never had anyone treated her so abominably, and yet she was sure she felt the hairs on her arm stand on end at his fiery touch. Her eyes met his, but she couldn't read his expression. The anger had retreated, but it had left nothing in its place.

"Sit down." It was a command, not a request. His hand still burning on her wrist, she had no choice but to return to her chair. When she had complied, Damon released her arm and went back to his own place at the head of the table. "Now," he said, "you've been running around in a tizzy since your arrival here. Can we discuss this like mature adults this time?"

Lowering her head a bit, Alex looked at him through her long lashes. "We can if you'll stop trying to overpower me—and invading my privacy!"

He sat down heavily in his chair. "I'm not mistreating you. If I were, you'd have more to complain about than you think you do, I assure you. And"—his voice seemed to vibrate with a low, angry hum—"if you're making reference to my entering your room, I apologized. Next time, if you don't want me to enter, speak up. Letti!" he yelled, forcing the brunt of his dissatisfaction on the hapless housekeeper. "Get dinner on the table."

Letti came hurrying through the swinging door and took scalloped potatoes and green beans from the tray she carried, placing them on the table. She left and returned with a plate of golden cornbread before Damon resumed his conversation. Letti sat down with them and Damon's eyes slanted momentarily at Alex. Staring defiantly back at him, she had no intention of giving up an inch of ground. She was furious at his hint that she had wanted him to enter her room. She couldn't be held responsible if he couldn't hear. Anyway, no other man would have come in without making sure he had been granted permission. For a moment she was afraid he might resort to violence, but he looked away from her abruptly.

Dinner began without conversation. Even Letti remained discreetly silent. The meal was well under way when Damon finally spoke. "Why can't you behave normally, like other girls your age? Secretarial skills are good for any woman. You don't intend to work all of your life, do you? Don't you want a husband, children, a home of your own?"

Alex tilted her head angrily. "By 'normal' you obviously mean only the women who conform to your ideas. Well, I am normal, thank you, for a woman my age. Of course I want husband, a home, and children, but I happen to be selective. I haven't found the man who can make me change my mind about a career. And women *can* have both. Or hasn't the news reached you yet down here in the South?"

"As far as I'm concerned, a woman can't have both," he stated coldly.

"And you don't have a woman, do you?" she asked with feigned sweetness. "Not a wife, at any rate," she added.

Shaking his head in frustration, he dropped his knife and glared at her. "Why do you want to work in the animal shelter if your career is so important to you?"

"I want to become a veterinarian, that's why. And in case you don't understand it, I need experience with animals."

Damon's handsome features registered total surprise. He looked at her for a full minute before replying. "I see. Aren't you being a bit optimistic? I didn't realize you had such high aspirations."

"I want to become a veterinarian, and I'm as able to do it as anyone else!" Was he implying that she wasn't intelligent enough for such a career?

"Are you?" he asked in a deep voice. "I understand the requirements are quite strict and the costs rather high. There's more to becoming a vet than simple desire." As if he were dismissing the topic, he looked down at his plate and resumed eating.

Irritated by his obviously low opinion of her, Alex fumed, "A person can do anything she sets her mind to. Where there's a will, there's a way, and I'm going to become a veterinarian! I'm an excellent student! I graduated with honors. And if you're concerned that I'll expect you to pay for my education when the costs are obviously going to be much higher than you anticipated, don't be! You don't need to supply me with anything! I'll manage on my own."

Damon cast brooding brown eyes in her direction. "One would think, Miss Hawthorne," he sneered, "that you had suddenly inherited a fortune. First you tell me you will replace a two-thousand-dollar chess set. Now you tell me you can finance an exorbitantly expensive education. It's extremely difficult to get into vet school, you know; there are only a limited number of veterinary colleges in this country. I happen to know the situation quite well. A friend of mine is in private practice. You would attend the University of Georgia, you know, as a Virginia resident."

Alex colored. He had hinted at expenses and problems she hadn't even suspected. She didn't know as much about the situation as he did. It seemed that she didn't know as much about it as anyone she spoke with and she was embarrassed by her lack of information, but she was determined not to be intimidated by Damon. "I'll get a loan," she retorted.

Damon chuckled softly. "You are a naive child. Really, Alex, I had other plans for you. Don't you think you might be interested in the secretarial school program and perhaps a course in small business management? I've been studying the recent reports of my company, and I—"

There! He had admitted it. He had made plans for her. "I've no doubt that you have plans for me," she interrupted him, "but I'm not impressed, not with your company or your plans! I'm not interested in attending your school. I want to become a veterinarian—not just another secretary. And you have no right to make plans for me anyway—any plans!"

Taking a deep breath, Damon made a conscious effort to control his anger. He stared at her for a few minutes before he spoke, and she noted with alarm the twitching of his jaw muscle. "For your information, a secretary these days is quite highly skilled. And you didn't wait for me to finish, Alex. I had a proposition that might have benefited you. Your father was obsessed with the secretarial schools. They were his idea. I never thought the idea would work, initially, not with other schools already in the same field, but your father had a dream that they could. If he hadn't gone in with me when I was twenty-one and helped me start the first school, I never would have been able to succeed. So you see, I owe your father a debt. And believe me, Miss Hawthorne, one way or another, I intend to repay it." He paused for a moment, glancing at Letti, who stared down at her plate. "I thought that we might be able to discuss your future as two sensible, rational human beings when you had settled in a bit. However, I can see how wrong I was." He placed his hands firmly on the table on either side of his plate as if bracing himself against some unpleasantness. "I see now that you have inherited your father's false pride, his foolish independence—and his self-inflated opinion!"

Alex trembled with wrath at hearing him insult her father's memory and herself so callously! "Are you quite finished?" she asked sharply. "Because if you are, I think I'll go now. It seems, Mr. Montaigne, that my coming here has been a dreadful mistake from the very start. I'll be out of your house in the morning."

A tight smile played across Damon's mouth. "I think

not, Miss Hawthorne. You and I made an agreement. You agreed to come here to live, at least until you're twenty-one, and I agreed to put you through college. I intend to live up to my end of the agreement—you'll get that education in veterinary medicine if that's what you really want—and I'll see that you live up to your end."

"You'll do no such thing!" she rasped, pushing her chair away so forcefully that it clattered to the floor. She turned on her heel and stalked angrily from the room. He had another thought coming if he thought he could order her around. She didn't care *who* he was!

Chapter Four

"Get back here, Alex!" Damon bellowed after her.

Yanking the door open, she marched into the hall, trembling with indignation. She heard a movement behind her, but she didn't turn around.

"Alex!" The harsh sound of her name caused her to shiver, but still she refused to look back as she ran up the steps. Her footsteps on the stairs sounded dreadfully loud, and she realized that there were heavier footsteps pounding ominously behind hers. When she cast a fleeting glance over her shoulder, she was astonished to see how closely Damon was following her—and how furious he looked.

She rushed down the hall to her room, flung open the door, then searched vainly for a few frantic seconds before she remembered that the door didn't have a lock.

Roadside, surprised by her sudden entrance, jumped up from his curled position on her bed, but Alex didn't have time to ponder his fate when her own was so clearly in jeopardy. Rushing to the closet to retrieve her old suitcase, she heard the door yanked open so hard that it banged against the wall.

Her heart fluttered dangerously as Damon, moving on lean, hard-muscled legs, closed the gap between them. His hands reached out to grab her wrists, causing her to drop the brown suitcase, which crashed noisily to the floor. Alex gasped audibly as her startled blue eyes, inches from Damon's fiery brown ones, flitted quickly over the strong, angular jaw. She noted the twitching muscle in his jaw with a feeling of despair.

"Let me go!" she demanded.

"What do you think you're doing?" he growled.

Trying to free herself from his cruel grip, Alex twisted and turned her wrists. In response, Damon pulled her closer, causing her breasts to brush his shirt.

The words Alex tried to summon caught in her throat. Her body seemed to be on fire where it had made contact with his; she felt breathless. "I won't stay here and be subjected to your insults," she managed to say. "I won't! I don't need you! I can take care of myself, thank you!"

"You are," he muttered harshly, "without a doubt, the most exasperating female I've ever encountered!" His blazing eyes peered down into her wide ones. "I've a good mind to turn you over my knee and blister your bottom!"

"You wouldn't dare!" she cried, twisting to one side so violently that the entire length of her body pressed against his. Did she imagine it, or did a strange look enter his eyes?

"Oh, Alex, Alex," he suddenly murmured deeply, "you're so innocent, so naive." His eyes searched her face, and he made no move to step away from the pressure of her body against his. He put his face close to hers—perilously close—and she sucked in her breath at his nearness. It seemed to Alex that she was about to be consumed by him. She had never been so over-whelmed by a man. She felt that this man, like the powerful pirates of yesterday, would be able to take what he wanted and discard the rest with no regard for the consequences. And she had the silliest notion that he wanted her. She held her breath and tried to quell the treachery of her heart. Surely she didn't want him too! His lips, so close, so full, so knowing, neared hers. His breath, smelling faintly of the heavy, sweet aroma of pipe tobacco, was hot on her cheek. Possessed of a will of their own, her lips betrayed her as they parted eagerly. She wanted his kiss. She could almost feel the touch of his mouth on hers, his lips were so near.

This impossible man who had insulted her so hatefully just a few minutes ago, this man who had ruined her father's life, this man who had mocked her and teased her since her arrival was going to kiss her—and she was going to let him. She knew it was insane, but she had never known such heady sensations, and it seemed the essence of injustice that this cruel man could tantalize her so.

Suddenly he bent his dark head and his lips closed possessively over hers as he gathered her hungrily in his arms, a half-groan sounding deep in his throat. The touch of his lips on hers seemed to spark a sleeping passion in her. Recklessly, she pressed her body to his, her arms wrapping tightly around his broad back as she responded with a wild abandon to the fire racing through her veins. She had never had much time for romance, but the kisses she had received before had never been like this.

She held him fiercely to her, wanting to feel every hard line of his muscled body against hers. In response, his fingers tightened on her back, digging into the flesh demandingly. His kiss deepened, and Alex heard a small moan come from her throat. As a shudder of desire went through her, she trembled violently in his arms.

As suddenly as the kiss had begun, it was over. Damon straightened abruptly, pulling away from her. Breathing rapidly, Alex felt as if she had received a slap in the face at his sudden withdrawal. He shoved his hands in his pockets as if the feel of her had burned him. "I'm sorry," he growled, his eyes glowing with banked fires. "It won't happen again."

Alex took a step backward, wiping a hand across her slightly swollen lips as she did so. Shame burning in her, she knew she had disappointed him. He had made a fool out of her. "I told you never to touch me again!" she croaked. "I shouldn't even be here." She was shocked and embarrassed that she had yielded so willingly to his touch.

As though he were angrier than ever, his eyes raked over her face before he unleashed a new tirade. "Your mother and I had an understanding, Alex. I am going to see to your future! Money is no object with me, and I'll see that you get your education in veterinary medicine if it's the last thing I do! You'll certainly never manage on your own. Undoubtedly, you don't even realize that you need preveterinary medicine to even enter veterinary college."

Alex's pulse was racing. Her head was spinning; her emotions were churning within her. She couldn't even remember what they were fighting about with Damon so close to her. She stared blankly at his lips.

"You'll need work experience. I'll get you a job with my friend who's a vet. Then we'll both see firsthand if you have what it takes or if you're simply chasing a childish dream."

In spite of the harshness of his words, Alex was suddenly all attention at the mention of the veterinarian. A smile played across her lips. "Brent Haggerman?"

Damon directed a surprised glance at her. "How did you know?"

"I met him at the shelter today. He was the veterinarian who treated Roadside, my kitten. Casaundra Calahan took me around and she introduced us. He's quite nice, your friend."

The look that crossed Damon's face was a peculiar one. "I see," he said. "I wasn't aware that you'd accomplished so much today." He eyed her briefly and his anger seemed to fade. "Well, if you're quite finished with your little temper tantrum, we'll finish dinner." Turning on his heel, he strode to the door.

"I was not having—" she began, but the slam of the door muffled her words.

The encounter with Damon had drained her, and she fell back on her bed, exhausted. After the fact, she felt rather ashamed of her behavior at the dinner table, but he *had* provoked her. A scarlet flush lit her cheeks as she thought about the way she had responded when he had kissed her. Shaking her head, she couldn't even bear to think about it. Anway, she was jubilant over his proposed plan for her to work with Brent, regardless of his reasons. But he had stated his intent with such animosity. . . .

Suddenly she wished that she hadn't been so quick to close the avenues of communication between them, but under the circumstances she'd had no choice. There were so many questions she had wanted to ask him, and she was curious now about the proposition he had intended to make to her. She sighed. Maybe it was for the best that things had worked out this way. Whatever the proposition was, it didn't matter now. He had made it quite painfully clear that he intended to see that she got her wish to go to veterinary college. Sighing, she left the room, making sure to close the door behind her, and went back down to dinner.

On Saturday morning Alex was surprised by a commanding knock on her door. This time she was quick to yell loudly, "Just a minute! Just a minute!" as she pulled on her robe. When she opened the door, she found Damon leaning against the door frame wearing a light blue pullover sweater and matching slacks that enhanced his devilishly dark good looks. Alex, still a little sleepy, made the foolish mistake of allowing her greedy eyes to take their fill of the man.

A mocking smile parted his lips. "Like what you see?"

Embarrassed that he had caught her staring, Alex insisted, "No! Of course not!" She was fully awake now. "What do you want?"

His smile vanished as rapidly as it had come. "I want to come in. What do you think I want?" he asked. "Am I imposing on you too much? Would you mind terribly if I came in? You have covered yourself adequately, have you not?"

She opened the door for him, her eyes on his broad back as he walked to her velvet chair and sat down. His virility made her feel breathless, and she thought he looked absurd on such a dainty chair. Tightening the belt of her robe, she returned to her bed and took Roadside in her arms. Daman cast a critical eye on the creature.

"We're going to Brent's animal clinic today to see about that job for you," he announced matter-of-factly. "You are still interested, aren't you? Or have you something else arranged for yourself? As fast as you get around, perhaps you've already talked to Brent about it." His eyes roved slowly over her as he spoke, and she couldn't help but remember how hungrily he had looked at her near-naked body when he was in her room that first night or how his lips had closed over hers when he had last been in her room. She felt her body respond to the interest in his brazen gaze, and she despised herself for the excitement his look could arouse in her. She was aware that Damon made an effort to annoy her in any way he could, but this bold survey of her body was the most disturbing of all.

"Of course I haven't spoken to him about it myself," she retorted. "I wouldn't dare usurp your authority, Mr. Montaigne," she insisted, placing heavy emphasis on his name.

His smile was taunting. "I see. Well—Miss Hawthorne—with you one never knows, does one? You're full of surprises—some of which aren't exactly pleasant."

"Just what do you mean by that?" She stared at him with wide eyes.

"Your appearance, for example," he nettled. "That slight but shapely, tempting, helpless little body hardly prepares one for the stubborn, slanted personality that erupts."

"Well, you certainly aren't a tower of goodness, just in case you've forgotten," she flared, cheeks flaming hotly. "That tall, forceful body hardly prepares one for the—"

He stood up quickly, scowling as he dismissed her with a wave of his hand. "I'm not here to exchange insults with you. If you want to ride with me to see Brent, get dressed and get your breakfast. You'll get the job regardless. I'm leaving at nine." Without further comment, he stalked out of the room.

Burning with anger, Alex jumped determinedly under the bedcovers. He hadn't even given her the chance to finish her sentence. She had wanted to confront him about her father, but he'd silenced her. Well, he'd said she would get the job regardless of whether she went or not, so why should she go? A few minutes ticked relentlessly by before she convinced herself that only she would be hurt if she didn't take the job with Brent. Becoming a veterinarian was what she wanted, and the experience would be invaluable to her. She certainly didn't want to remain in Damon's house any longer than necessary. And if she was going to take the job, she might as well be in on the arrangements. Resignedly, she bathed and slipped into a long-sleeved navy blue sweater and light blue wool pants. The combination set off her eyes, and she was pleased with the image she saw in her mirror.

When she entered the dining room, Damon was

sitting at the table sipping a steaming cup of coffee as he idly read the paper. Alex decided against breakfast. "I'm ready," she remarked, trying to muster a smile for him.

"I'm not." Not even looking up at her, he continued to turn the pages of his newspaper while she sat down across from him and tried to keep from speaking to him in kind.

In his own good time, he stood up and, without saying a word, walked from the room. Slowly, Alex trailed along behind him out of the house. She gasped as she stepped out on the porch to see a storybook winter. The rains of the previous evening had left frozen mementos everywhere she looked. Huge icicles were hanging like stalactites from the roof of the porch. Each and every limb of the weeping willow trees was encased in ice; they were twinkling like jewels in the early morning sunlight. Even the leaves of the magnolia trees were captured in an icy stillness. George Willis was cleaning the ice off the driveway with a shovel, a bag of salt, and some ashes.

Alex followed Damon as he stepped out on the grass to crunch his way toward the driveway. Entranced by the novelty of all this, she tramped down on the lawn, then looked back at her footprints remaining in the crushed ice behind her.

As she turned to step onto the pavement of the driveway, her foot, finding no traction on a tiny patch of almost invisible ice, shot out from under her. She uttered a startled cry of surprise and protest.

Damon turned, and hands like hot iron whipped out to grab her, catching her securely under her arms. To Alex, his hands seemed to sear through her clothing. The masculine smell of after-shave lotion, inches away, teased her nostrils in the crisp air.

Stunned, Alex stared up into Damon's brooding eyes, thinking for just an instant that she saw concern there as her heart thudded loudly beneath his hands.

Just as quickly as he had rescued her, he released her, plunking her down solidly on the driveway and clenching his hands into fists.

"For Pete's sake, Alex, watch out for the icy patches before you hurt yourself!"

The words of gratitude she had intended to say turned bitter in her mouth. He acted as if she'd wanted to slip on the ice. Did he think she wanted his attentions? Her eyes shot up to meet his cold ones. "Don't worry about me, Damon. I can take care of myself, thank you!"

She slowed her pace as he turned on his heel to walk the remaining steps to the garage. Opening the door to reveal three expensive cars housed there, he went to a burgundy Porsche and stepped inside. Contemptuously noting the lack of manners that Southern gentlemen were supposed to be famous for, Alex climbed in on the other side. Damon took a key from his key ring and thrust it toward her before starting the car. "You'll be needing transportation. I assume you do drive."

Trying to remain civil, Alex flushed as her eyes roamed to the two other less pretentious cars. "I drive very well," she stated, "but one of the others will do, thank you."

"You don't care for this one?" he asked tersely.

"Yes, of course."

"Then use it."

Alex shrugged in resignation and turned her eyes from his. She listened to the clink of the tire chains as Damon backed out of the garage and drove down the driveway. In moments, her anger dissipated as she marveled at the countryside. Telephone wires laden with ice dipped between the poles; tree limbs, bent to the ground under icy weight, were stretched to the breaking point. Never had Alex seen such chilly beauty. Along the way, a few cars without chains had slid helplessly off the road. Alex was full of questions and comments, but Damon made no attempt at conversation in return, so she fell silent.

She was relieved when he stopped in front of a long, low brick building snuggled beneath two large trees on the outskirts of town. The letters on an icy sign proclaimed BRENT HAGGERMAN, D.V.M., and listed office hours. Damon stepped out of the car and Alex, having no illusions that he would open her door, got out quickly on her side. She followed him as he walked carefully up the walk and entered the building. Moving quickly between the rows of owners holding cats and dogs to greet the front office girl warmly, he went, unannounced, into the next room, where Brent was wiping a metal table clean before he saw his next patient.

"Hello," he said pleasantly, looking up at Alex and Damon with bright blue eyes. "What brings you two out to this neck of the woods so early?" His face was friendly and his boyish smile was warm as he looked at them.

"I understand you've met Miss Hawthorne," Damon said, nodding to Alex.

Brent smiled appreciatively at her. "Yes, we've met. How are you today, Alex? You look just fine."

Grateful that someone seemed genuinely happy to see her, Alex returned his generous smile. "I am fine, thank you, Brent."

"Alex wants to work for you, Brent," Damon broke in. "It can be arranged, can't it?"

Alex was momentarily alarmed by the look on Brent's face. She didn't understand his brief flash of hostility. Again she wondered if she were reading something into a situation that simply wasn't there, but Brent's sharp words about Damon the day Casaundra had introduced them rushed to her mind. Brent looked at her, his eyes solemn for just a few seconds, before he turned to Damon. His voice was surprisingly warm.

"Yes, I'm sure it can be arranged. You know my practice is mixed. I have certain office hours and set surgery hours, but I'm always on call for farm animal emergencies." Placing a hand to his chin, he stroked it thoughtfully. "I have a young man who assists me on Mondays and Wednesdays. The office is closed on Thursdays and Sundays, though I'm always on call. I can use Alex on Tuesdays, Friday nights, and Saturdays."

"Oh, thank you. That would be great!" Alex was unable to contain her enthusiasm. "I really do appreciate this." Instinctively, she held out her hand to him.

Taking it in his, Brent bowed to her. "Don't mention it. It will be my pleasure, I'm sure." He ignored Damon's stern look. "I'm always glad to be of assistance to a beautiful lady." The brief stroking he gave her hand before releasing it didn't go unnoticed by the sharp-eyed Damon.

"That's settled," Damon remarked with finality. "I have other business today, so see you later, Brent." He strode brusquely from the room without additional comment.

"This Friday?" Alex inquired of Brent, eyes aglow, his peculiar first reaction forgotten. "Shall I come this Friday?"

He grinned at her. "Yes, about three thirty. We're open until seven thirty."

Damon's dark head suddenly reappeared in the doorway. "How about that play in Greensboro Thursday night, Brent? I have tickets for all of us. See you at my place about seven?"

"You know I'd love it." Brent's eyes settled easily on Alex's face as he spoke.

Without another word, Damon disappeared again.

"I really do appreciate this, Brent," Alex murmured.

"Think nothing of it. Anyway"—his smile was ironic—"how could I refuse? Damon financed this building for me."

Somewhat taken aback by this information, Alex gave him a nervous smile before hurrying after Damon. So that was why Damon had been so sure she'd get the job!

When she climbed into the car beside him, the engine was already idling and she was aware that he was in his usual ill humor. She resolved to remain quiet in the hope of not annoying him further, even though the idea of her new job had her excited and eager to talk.

They were well under way when Damon turned to look at her. "Are you always so familiar with strangers?" he asked coolly.

"What do you mean?" A little of the hurt she felt seeped into her voice. Nothing she did seemed to satisfy this impossible man. He had no right to treat her as he did.

"I mean," he said, staring at her from beneath lowered eyelids, "the way you grabbed for Brent's hand when he said you could come to work for him."

"I didn't grab for his hand!" she protested indignantly. "I—I wanted him to know how much I appreciated his kindness in giving me the chance to work at the clinic."

"I see," he mused. "And how will you show me your appreciation for offering my home, my financial support for your education, and my friends to assist you in your plans, Alex? How much is it all worth? Surely more than hand-holding."

Alex was so shocked by the implication of his words that she could think of no response. The night he had barged into her room and caught her almost naked came suddenly to her mind. Had she been right in what she had thought about him? Did he think—could he possibly think—was he implying that she should let him . . .? Shaking with fury, she stared out the window at the passing frosted fields of the countryside. Just let him dare to lay a hand on her! She'd show him how she would repay him! She'd give him more than hand-holding. She'd give him something that he'd never forget!

She was so furious with him that she didn't even notice the smile that twisted his lips as he drove along.

They turned off the road onto a winding lane that stopped in front of a fabulous house that had been converted into some sort of business. The facade was very attractively done in white stonework, and the surrounding grounds were pleasant. The ice was already melting in the morning sun, Alex noted, looking at the high boxwood hedging that fenced in the property and the huge holly bushes that brightened the front with clusters of scarlet berries. Several smaller buildings matching the facade of the main building were scattered over the property, the icicles that hung from them dripping in the sunlight.

"This is the secretarial school. I'll show you around," Damon explained, getting out of the car.

Alex rapidly scrambled out. Damon was already starting up the steps, and she hurried along after him, hating him for his arrogant disregard for her comfort. Exasperated, she called after him, "If you intend to show me around, at least have the courtesy to wait for me!"

A smile touching his lips, he crossed his arms and stopped. "I am sorry," he said in an amused voice. "I really thought you were so self-sufficient, Miss Hawthorne, that you would shun any display of courtesy on my part."

Ignoring his caustic remark, Alex flipped a strand of blond hair over her shoulder and caught up with him. He pulled out his pipe and idly tamped some tobacco into it before applying the match. When he didn't resume walking, Alex went past him. Damon stood staring after her for a few moments until he saw her approach the front door and look around in dismay. She didn't know where to go from there, and she was forced to wait for him to come to her.

Saying nothing as he approached, Damon walked over to her and leisurely opened the door for her to enter. "At your service, madam," he said at length, flashing her a big smile.

"Thank you," was her curt reply. She marched inside and stood by the receptionist's desk.

"Mr. Montaigne," the pleasant-faced young woman remarked, "how nice to see you. I thought you were in New York setting up the new school."

Damon's smile was warm. "That was my plan, Nealy, but the weather had something else in mind, so I postponed the trip."

"Shall I ring Miss Calahan for you?"

"No, I'll go to her. I want to show this . . . young lady . . . around."

Nealy's smile was immediately professional. "Are you thinking of enrolling in our program?" Her voice became a well-trained blend of business and friendliness in the presence of a prospective customer.

Damon answered before Alex had the chance. "Oh, definitely not. Miss Hawthorne wouldn't dream of becoming a lowly secretary." A mocking smile curved his lips, and he cocked his head in Alex's direction. To her disgust, she felt herself bristling. He had the most maddening way of putting her on the spot.

The receptionist's expression was puzzled, but she made no further comment.

"Where can I find Miss Calahan?" Damon asked.

"I think she's in with the business machines. One of the machines isn't working properly, and we had to call in a repairman. I believe Miss Calahan is still with him."

"Thanks, Nealy." With long strides, Damon moved down a hall to his left.

"Oh, Mr. Montaigne," Nealy called, hurrying after him, "my niece is coming to visit me this weekend; you remember Debbi, the thirteen-year-old. May we ride your horses if the weather is good?"

"Sure, Nealy. Anytime. You just tell George that I said it was all right."

"Thanks a lot," she exclaimed, her face lightening up. "You're an angel."

An angel! Alex thought. How could anyone call Damon an angel? Trailing along behind him, she told herself it was incredible. She had several names for him herself, but *angel* certainly wasn't one of them.

As she looked around the school, she had to admit that she was strangely pleased that he was showing her around. The school had been her father's dream, and even though he hadn't accomplished it himself, it was nice to know that the dream had come true. Looking in some of the rooms as she passed, she couldn't help but wonder how different her parents' lives would have been if they had remained in Danville and had become successful along with Damon Montaigne. And again she wondered why they hadn't.

They entered a room filled with young women. In the back of the room, Casaundra, clothed in a sophisticated red jersey dress, was bending intently over a copy machine as a blue-uniformed man worked. Walking quietly up behind her, Damon put a hand on her back. The startled look in her big violet eyes only made them more appealing as they lifted to his.

"Why, Damon! I thought you were in New York!" Putting both her elegant hands on his arms, she allowed her eyes to roam over his face. "It's wonderful to see you, of course, but what happened to the trip? Are you all right?"

"I'm fine. I got snowed out of New York, so the trip had to be postponed." As he smiled engagingly into the beautiful face, Alex could see that he cared for the tall, dark beauty, and a strange feeling crept over her. Damon had never smiled at her that way. He rarely smiled at her at all unless he was taunting her.

"Come into my office," Casaundra invited gaily.

"I'm through here. The repairman can finish up."
Pursing her red lips, she murmured, "I just wish I were
mechanically inclined. Some of the problems with these
machines are so uncomplicated once one sees what's
wrong with them, but I just don't have a talent for
repairs. It would save you so much money." She batted
her long, sooty lashes at Damon, and Alex was shocked
to see her behave so coyly. This was certainly a
different side of the strong, haughty, capable woman
she had met yesterday.

Alex was even more surprised to see Damon snap at
the bait, though she told herself she shouldn't have
been. "You do more than enough for me," he said. "I
don't know what I would do without you."

A smile of pure delight brightened Casaundra's face.
"You say such nice things to me, boss."

Alex checked a foolish urge to mimic the honeyed
purr of Casaundra's husky voice.

With Alex following the other two, they went to
Casaundra's well-furnished office, where Damon and
Alex seated themselves on a low red velvet couch while
Casaundra poured coffee from a graceful monogramed
pot. Like the woman, the room was a smooth mixture
of elegance and efficiency. An assortment of pictures
lined the walls and others were situated on the large
brown desk, but Alex looked away when she spied a
picture of Damon and Casaundra beaming brightly at
her.

"And how are you today, Alex?" Casaundra asked,
picking just that moment to finally acknowledge her
presence. "I met your guest the other day, Damon,"
she said, turning liquid violet eyes on him.

Alex never had the chance to respond to Casaundra's
greeting. Once again Damon cut her off before she
could utter a word. "So I heard," he replied, the
friendliness he had shown Casaundra quickly evaporat-
ing as he turned his dark eyes to Alex. "I would have

thought Alex could have waited until we discussed her plans before charging all over creation getting into trouble."

Casaundra's vaguely unhappy look was that of a small child unjustly chastised. "Getting into trouble?" The purr started to work in her voice like a car engine warming up.

"You took her to the shelter, Casaundra. I told you I had other plans for Alex. It was stupid of her to hunt for a job on her second day here. And if that wasn't bad enough, that wretched animal she lugged home broke my glass chess set."

"Damon, no! I hope you don't blame me." Casaundra turned her gaze to Alex, and her eyes were anything but pretty as they glared warningly at her. "Alex so had her heart set on going to the pound that I felt I couldn't refuse her. I had no way of knowing she hadn't discussed her plans with you or, of course, I wouldn't have taken her. And she insisted on taking that poor unfortunate animal home with her. I certainly didn't think it was my place to tell your guest what she could or couldn't do. Why, that would have been so rude!" The sweet voice was empty of the blatant spite that played in the dancing eyes.

Alex was taken aback by Casaundra's words. She was almost too surprised to reply. Looking hesitantly at Damon for a few seconds, she tried to think of a response. Things weren't quite as the conniving Casaundra had made them appear, but Alex *had* made the final decision to take the kitten to Willowstone, and it was true that she had wanted to go to the shelter. "I'm fully accountable for my actions," she said in a tight little voice.

"I'm well acquainted with Alex's obstinacy," Damon replied evenly. As he looked at Casaundra, his smile returned. "I've already witnessed her regrettable lack of control, so, of course, I don't hold you responsible for her behavior."

Of course not! Alex thought resentfully. So he's witnessed my regrettable lack of control, has he? He was certainly the most horrible man she had ever had the misfortune to encounter, and she wanted desperately to give him a piece of her mind. Instead, she stared into the blackness of her coffee and ruefully thought that the woman had manipulated her, just as she was able, apparently, to manipulate Damon. Casaundra had been sure Alex would fall into Damon's disfavor if she took a job at the shelter or took the kitten home, even though she had no way of knowing the damage Roadside would do. She had deliberately worked the situation to her advantage and helped Alex make a fool of herself. In the future, Alex vowed to be more wary of the spiteful woman's assistance.

Neither Damon nor Alex spoke when they returned to the car and left the school. Alex had nothing she wished to say and Damon was apparently of the same mind. They had ridden some distance before he said, shattering the silence, "How about some lunch?"

She stared at him, unwilling to believe that he was actually being nice to her.

His sudden smile caused her breath to catch in her throat. "You didn't eat breakfast, and I know a wonderful little Italian restaurant. They serve the best manicotti in the state. Do you like Italian food?"

"Yes," Alex replied with guarded politeness. She did, in fact, love Italian food, especially manicotti, but she was leery of Damon's overture.

"Good. I know you won't be disappointed. These people came here from Italy a couple of years ago, so the food is authentic." He made a left-hand turn and they were at the restaurant in minutes.

Alex opened her car door and was waiting when Damon walked around the car to escort her into the charming restaurant. Quaintly decorated with small tables covered in red oilcloth and tall chairs, the walls painted with scenes of romantic gondolas in the canals of Venice and the ruins of Rome, the room was cheerful and cozy.

Alex was surprised when Damon, smiling in a way that made her heart beat faster, pulled out a chair so she could sit down. She was even more surprised when he began to discuss the menu with her. After several minutes, they decided on an antipasto, manicotti, and a carafe of red wine.

While Damon gave the waiter the order, Alex watched him surreptitiously. She suddenly found herself thinking the most ridiculous thoughts as she sat across from this self-assured, handsome, arrogant man. She could understand what Casaundra saw in him; he could be incredibly and deceptively charming when he wanted to be.

She blushed when he looked at her and caught her observing him. He stared at her speculatively for a moment before he spoke. "Well, has the city changed much, Alex?" he asked at length. "Or is it as you remember it?"

She shrugged lightly. "Actually, I don't remember much of it. It seems so long ago that I lived here, and I guess the physical characteristics of the city weren't of much importance to me."

"Do you think you might like to settle down here now?" he asked, his strangely soft voice causing her to search his face with inquisitive eyes.

Why was her heart pounding so savagely? She didn't understand the churning emotions that rose inside her at the simple question. "I don't know," she murmured. "I haven't thought much about it."

"Think about it," he said quietly, his dark eyes coaxing.

Alex felt breathless and confused by his request, but she was sorry when the waiter suddenly stepped up to their table with the wine.

Damon poured a glass for each of them, and the conversation moved on to the general area and the secretarial schools. Alex waited expectantly, hoping Damon would say something more about her staying in Danville, but she was disappointed. They ate their meal slowly, both of them seeming quite willing to linger there in the restaurant and savor one of the few times that they had spent peacefully in each other's company.

The meal ended much too soon for Alex, and in a short time they were back in the car and once again on their way to Willowstone. When Damon turned into the driveway a few minutes later, he asked casually, "Do you ride, Alex?"

"A little," she replied quickly. When the silence threatened to settle in again, she asked, "How many horses do you have? I've heard them in the stable."

"Three fine bay mares and a black stallion—Spanish-Barbs. We'll have to get up early one morning and I'll show you the grounds."

He smiled again, and Alex hated the way the sight of his smile caused her heart to jump. She felt like kicking herself. What on earth was wrong with her? Nothing had changed between the two of them just because Damon had condescended to be nice to her for a single hour. Why was her silly heart fluttering this way? Why couldn't Damon either be completely nice or coldly nasty to her, and why couldn't her foolish heart follow her mind's example and despise the man?

Chapter Five

The days until Thursday passed with Alex and Damon
coexisting, if not peacefully, then at least tolerantly.
Somehow Alex never found just the right time to
confront Damon about her father, and the longer she
waited, the more reluctant she was to bring up such an
unpleasant subject. She did, however, think often of
the file cabinet in his room. When she had showered
and dressed Thursday morning, she walked past
Damon's room and found the door open. Her heartbeats increased rapidly as she boldly peered inside. She
didn't see him anywhere. By this time he had usually
left the house. Impulsively, she started to step inside,
overcome with curiosity about the school records, but
at the last moment she changed her mind. She had to be
sure that Damon was already gone.

Hurrying down the stairs, she found the dining room
empty. "Where's Damon?" she asked Letti as the
woman served her a cup of coffee, eggs, and toast.

"He already had breakfast—some time ago," Letti
explained.

"Oh," Alex murmured. Then surely he had left the
house. She toyed with her breakfast for a few minutes,
then excused herself. Once and for all, she was going to
satisfy her curiosity about those records. She practically

ran back up the steps to his room, afraid that if she delayed a second longer she would lose her nerve. Softly, she sneaked into his room and closed the door behind her. Her heart pounding savagely against her rib cage, she looked all around, then walked determinedly to the file cabinet and swiftly jerked open the first drawer. There was nothing in it but current records, and Alex quickly skipped to the next drawer, then the next, finding the previous years' records as she moved lower down the line.

"Darn," she muttered in frustration. There were stacks of records in each drawer, but it began to look like what she was hoping for wasn't there. Then, just when she was ready to give up and leave the room, she found the year she was searching for. Damon had kept the records all the way back to the beginning of the partnership. She saw her father's name listed with Damon's in the very bottom drawer. Squatting down on her heels, she pulled the drawer out with shaking fingers. To her bitter disappointment, when she flipped through the folder there was nothing to indicate the reason for the dissolution of the partnership.

"Darn!" she muttered again. She had taken a chance for nothing, and she'd been lucky she hadn't been caught snooping. She certainly wouldn't have been able to explain it. She had just started to put the records back in the drawer when she sensed, rather than heard, someone's presence. She didn't know who it could be other than Letti but, heart hammering, temples pounding, she didn't dare turn around. She stayed where she was, frozen in her crouched position. When she heard the heavy, ominous footsteps coming from Damon's bathroom, her heart sank and she was forced to turn her head. She had guessed wrong; he was still here!

Her eyes still level with the bottom drawer, she focused on a pair of dark shoes. Involuntarily, her eyes rose slowly, seeing a pair of muscular legs clad in dark slacks, a slim pair of hips, a broad chest with dark hair curling over its naked expanse, a strong neck, and, finally, a dark, scowling face. On seeing Damon's cold brown eyes, her blue ones blinked twice as she tried to meet his gaze.

"What, may I ask, are you doing?" he demanded, glaring down at her.

Alex's first impulse was to run, and she discarded the folder that was still in her hand with just that intention, but Damon bent down to her and fingers of steel grasped both her wrists to drag her up from the floor.

Straightening to her full height, dwarfed by his towering frame, she valiantly tried to meet his eyes. "I'm looking for information about my father," she retorted defiantly.

"And did you find what you were looking for?" he asked sharply.

She met his penetrating gaze for only a moment, then her eyes lowered and she unwillingly stared at his bronzed, muscled chest. She could feel the quickened rise and fall of her breathing and there was a tenseness in her stomach. She swallowed nervously, conscious of his eyes on her. She couldn't seem to think rationally with him standing so close to her, the scent of his after-shave strong in her nostrils.

"Alex," he growled, "did you find what you were looking for?"

"No," she declared confusedly, his nearness causing her heart to flutter wildly. She couldn't seem to control her thoughts with him so dangerously near. She couldn't even seem to remember what she was looking for, or why she had taken such a chance, stealing into his room. Her gaze met his again, and their eyes locked. Alex felt suddenly breathless. She wanted to turn away and she tried to free herself from his burning grasp, but he suddenly pulled her against him. She gasped with surprise as she found herself trapped against his naked chest. The tension in the heavily charged atmosphere increased with each passing second. Tipping her head back, Damon stared down into her eyes, and his lips swiftly descended to claim hers in a hard kiss. Alex couldn't seem to control her reactions. Remembering the first kiss he had given her and the way he had pulled away from her, Alex tried to resist him, ordering her body not to respond, but it was useless. Damon crushed her ruthlessly against his hard form, molding her hips to his strong thighs and she rose up on tiptoe to meet his possessive embrace. Her arms automatically encircled his neck and she increased the pressure of her mouth on his. The force of his lips against hers lessened and the kiss became a tantalizing, hungry caress, which Alex matched with a passionate response of her own. The feeling of his naked skin under her fingers as her hands trailed down his back sent her senses reeling. There was a yearning inside her that she had never known before. She was responding totally to Damon's fiery touch when he suddenly shoved her away with a smothered expletive.

Breathing raggedly, his voice hoarse, he demanded harshly, "Get out of here before you find more than you're looking for!"

Stunned, Alex stared at him a moment before a scarlet flush crept up her neck. Her pulse racing, her heart beating wildly, she backed away from him. Reaching blindly for the doorknob, she yanked the door open and escaped on flying feet. She quickly snatched her purse from her room and then dashed madly down the steps. She didn't stop running until she reached the car. Climbing into its relative safety, she sat for several moments, waiting for her crazy heart to stop beating so savagely. She despised Damon Montaigne! She had no idea why she reacted so strongly to his very nearness! She couldn't seem to control her emotions when he touched her; she couldn't even seem to think straight.

Not knowing what else to do, but wanting to get as far away from Damon as possible, she drove around until she found the new city library, and then, trying desperately to keep her thoughts off Damon, she forced herself to pass the time reading about Danville's history. In uncovering the history of the town she became enthralled with the history of Virginia in general, and at last her mind concentrated on something besides the feverish way she had felt in Damon's arms.

She discovered that Virginia had been the first of the English colonies to be established; very few of the settlers had lived through the first winter, and without the help of the Indians, none would have survived. Alex was interested to learn that the Indians were already growing tobacco, Danville's big crop, when the colonists arrived. Tobacco provided the colonists with both an export crop and a means of existing in the new land. It was so important that it became the basis for Virginia's entire structure and created the need for slaves, who helped the landowners become prosperous enough to build the elegant mansions that Virginia was so famous for. Ultimately, the slave system had been the cause of the demise of the gracious Southern way of life.

With reluctance, Alex left history and the library to be home in time for dinner and the play. She didn't relish the idea of facing Damon again, but it couldn't be avoided, and she was far from eager to go to the play. If just Brent had been going with them she would have been more enthusiastic, but Damon had informed her yesterday that Casaundra was joining them. The prospect of Casaundra's company on top of the morning's events gave Alex an uneasy feeling.

Dinner wasn't pleasant, but she managed to endure Damon's cool, aloof manner, and finally she escaped to her room. She was just stepping out of the tub when she heard the doorbell ring. It was only six, and she hadn't expected the guests to arrive until seven. She had wanted to look her best and had anticipated an hour in which to get ready. Wrapped in a towel, she went to open her door a crack so she could hear the voices downstairs. She heard Damon speak to both Brent and Casaundra; they must have arrived together. And Alex wasn't even dressed.

Anxiety rose in her. She could almost picture Casaundra, though she couldn't see her, and she was sure the tall beauty would be exquisitely attired. Alex hurried to her own closet to scan her few nice dresses. Pulling out a below-the-knee dress of soft baby blue velvet, she searched for the matching shoes. She had purchased the outfit for a special college event, but since her mother's health had worsened, she had never gotten to wear it. The shoes hadn't even been broken in. She had wanted to curl her hair, but now she wouldn't have time. Slipping into dainty lace underwear and nylons, she faced herself in the mirror with sudden despair. She had wanted to look good tonight, and the early arrival of the guests had robbed her of that luxury.

Piling her long blond hair on top of her head, she caught it with nearly invisible pins. The effect was good, and she let a few tendrils stray around her face. That looked even better, giving her the illusion of height and sophistication and exposing her delicate bone structure. She put on dark mascara and her wide blue eyes instantly became dramatic and deeply alluring. Dusted with a light powder, the freckles on her nose became invisible. She colored her lips with a deep rose lipstick.

When she stepped into the fitted dress, she was astonished at the transformation. She was sure the dress hadn't looked that good on her when she had purchased it, but her curves had matured a bit more since then. The vee neck was demure, yet still plunging enough to expose the swell of her generous breasts. The color of the dress, so well suited to that of her eyes, caused them to sparkle like two blue diamonds. She slid her small feet into the three-inch heels and smiled at the reflection of the beautiful, cosmopolitan lady that beamed at her. Her dressing had been much quicker than she intended, but it had more than accomplished the desired result. A bit uneasy on the tall shoes, she hurried down the stairs.

She was sure her legs were trembling when she approached the open door of the living room. Damon, Brent, and Casaundra were enjoying drinks by the warmth of the dazzling fire in the red-brick fireplace. Alex walked in and all conversation ceased as the three people focused on her with varying degrees of surprise. Brent and Casaundra sat on the settee and Damon stood by the fireplace. "Good evening," Alex offered a little too gaily.

Brent whistled softly. "Good evening to you, lovely, enchanting creature," he murmured, admiration obvious in the huskiness of his voice.

"Alex," Casaundra acknowledged, unguarded jealousy evident in her eyes. The purr of her feminine voice was working overtime, and Alex had the notion that she was angrier and more dangerous now than she had ever been before.

With a shock, she realized that it was Damon she really wanted to impress, and he simply stood mute, unsmiling, slowly spinning the brandy in his glass as his sharp eyes appraised her thoughtfully. Dashingly dressed in maroon slacks and a deeper maroon jacket, he seemed even more handsome than usual. After a moment, he spoke. "Would you like a drink?"

"I . . . yes, thank you." She wouldn't give him the satisfaction of knowing she had never had anything but wine.

"What would you like?"

Alex's brain raced furiously, but nothing came to mind.

"Perhaps a touch of sherry would be good on such a cold night," Brent suggested, smiling at her. "Let me get it, Damon."

She returned his smile. "Thank you, Brent. That sounds fine." Looking triumphantly at Damon, she was unable to miss the look of ridicule in his smoldering eyes as they climbed from her high-heeled shoes to the top of her high-piled blond hair, lingering briefly on her hips and cleavage on the way up.

Just as Brent crossed the room from the bar to where she stood, Alex saw a rush of fur as Roadside sneaked into the room. Shutting her eyes briefly to steel herself against Damon's fury, she realized that, in her haste, she must have left the door of her bedroom open. Roadside had remained either in her room or outside in the yard since the disastrous day when he had broken Damon's glass chess pieces. Of all the times for him to show himself again, he couldn't have chosen one more apt to humiliate her.

The others had seen his entry and Brent handed her the small glass of sherry and called out to him. "Here, kitty. Here, kitty, kitty, kitty."

Alex didn't dare look at Damon as Brent coaxed the little animal forward. With wide-eyed curiosity, he approached the gentle voice that called, but when Brent reached for him, Roadside made a mad dash around the room. Alex closed her eyes again, unwilling to look disaster in the face.

Instead, she felt it. Tiny claws grabbed familiarly at her leg, wrapping themselves about her ankle in a playful gesture. Alex didn't need to look down at her nylon to know that a run was rushing up her leg beneath Roadside's clutching paws.

Brent came to her rescue again. "Affectionate little

thing, isn't he? I'm glad to see him so frisky and happy. The little guy was sure a mess the first time I saw him. Here, let me take your sherry while you unwrap him."

Only the slight tremble of Alex's hand betrayed the taut stretch of her nerves as she smiled gratefully at Brent. "Thank you. I'll be just a minute. I'll put him away, repair the damage, and be right back."

"By all means, change your nylon now that the animal has destroyed it," Damon spoke out smoothly, "but leave the little charmer here. He does prove amusing, doesn't he?"

Alex gave him a hard look as she reached down to disentangle Roadside's claws before setting him on the floor. Head tilted, she rose and walked stiffly from the room. She was sure she could hear Casaundra's soft, deep laughter behind her, but when she reached the steps, the laughter changed to a startled shriek.

Unable to resist, Alex looked back to see Roadside complete his charge on Casaundra as he dashed up her dress and across the back of the settee to the floor, tumbling Casaundra's drink over the front of her peach frock in the process.

Suppressing shock and a threatening giggle, Alex hastened on her way up the steps, listening to the commotion behind her. She could hear Casaundra's angry exclamations, Letti's soothing assistance, and Damon's sharp rage.

"Alex! Alex! Get this cat out of here!" he bellowed from below. But she continued on her way. After all, he had told her to leave "the little charmer" there.

With a mixture of humiliation and humor, Alex dropped down on her bed for just a moment to regain her composure. It would take a bit of courage to return to the living room. As she put a hand to her head, she heard a heavy step on the stairs. "Alex! Alex!"

Fear caused her stomach to lurch wildly for just a second while she fought for control. She quickly got up from the bed, slipped off her shoes, and began to peel her nylon down her shapely thigh, hesitating only when Damon flung the door open and stared brazenly at her leg.

"You still haven't learned to wait for permission to enter a lady's bedroom," she snapped, letting her dress hem drop to cover her leg. Unthinkingly, she had expected him not to enter when he knew she would be changing, but she should have known better. That hadn't prevented him the first time.

"Do you know what that cat of yours has done now?" he asked, ignoring her sarcasm.

She widened her eyes. "You mean besides ruin my nylon?"

"You know perfectly well I mean besides ruin your nylon! That animal's damaged Casaundra's dress with his claws and spilled her drink on it!"

"No!" Pretended shock enlivened her face before she added coolly, "Then he did prove amusing, didn't he?"

Incensed, Damon stalked to where she stood and glowered at her. "Don't play with me, Alex. The dress will have to be replaced."

Alex stared back at him, refusing to be intimidated. She would have returned Roadside to her room, but Damon had told her to leave him, so how dare he bully her? "Put it on my bill along with the chessmen," she said crossly. "Now, if you'll excuse me, I have to change my stockings."

She reached for a new pair, but his hands lashed out to grab her shoulders, biting cruelly into her flesh. "I should march you down the stairs and make you apologize to Casaundra!"

Painfully, she wrenched away from him. "You wouldn't dare!"

"Don't tempt me!" With incredible swiftness, he yanked her forward, causing her to stumble as he crushed her unmercifully against his body. Uncertain of his intentions, she gasped as he stared down into her eyes. There was a burning glow in his, and for a moment Alex thought his lips were descending to meet hers.

Suddenly, he shook her roughly as if she were a small rag doll before pushing her away. "Oh, get out of my sight." He groaned deeply.

Alex stood still, astonished, shoulders burning where angry fingers had bitten into them, as he strode toward the door. "What do you want from me?" she demanded in a high voice. "Why have you brought me here? Wasn't it enough that you destroyed my father? Are you trying to destroy me, too?"

But the door slammed on her bitter words. It wasn't until Letti entered with the struggling Roadside that Alex could force herself to move from the spot where she stood.

"You ought to hurry, child," Letti cautioned her. "The play starts at eight. Greensboro is about an hour away, and now you'll have to stop by Casaundra's house so she can change."

Throwing Letti an unhappy look, Alex hurried to get ready, but she wished the others had gone without her. The evening had already proven to be worse than she had anticipated. She had the feeling she'd already endured a play this evening—and she had been the main character.

Alex lay in her bed watching the room lighten with the first hint of dawn. She had survived the previous evening, but only because Brent had chosen to treat her with the consideration of a man genuinely concerned for her comfort. Casaundra, freshly attired, had seemed intent on showing Alex that both men were hers by bestowing a portion of her attention on Brent along with the generous serving she gave to Damon. At the same time, she had deliberately spurned Alex.

Damon was much too busy showering his charms on

Casaundra to pay Alex much attention, and he seemed to resent Brent's attention to her when he did notice her. At least if she remained in her bed, she might not have to face his cruel taunts this morning. He seemed to have had a few barbs on the tip of his tongue last night when she excused herself for bed, but mercifully he hadn't released them.

Her spirits began to brighten considerably when she remembered that this afternoon was her first day to work with Brent. She tried to think of what she would wear to the clinic and decided on multicolored slacks that wouldn't show dirt or hair too easily. Dismissing last night's leftover moodiness, she hopped out of bed and checked her closet. She chose what she wanted and hooked the hangers over the dainty dressing screen. Then she took a leisurely bath and climbed into jeans and a blue plaid shirt to face the morning.

The sun was just starting to brighten the night sky with shadowy hues of blue and brilliant pink when Alex peeked out her window before going down to breakfast. Opening her door, she could tell Letti was up; the wonderful smell of fresh perked coffee filled the hall with a rich, mellow aroma. Alex was beginning to feel good about the new day when she entered the dining room.

"Well, Miss Hawthorne." Damon's deep voice caught her unprepared. "What brings you from your bed at this decent hour of the morning?"

Taking a long breath, Alex determined not to be stung into returning his taunt. "Breakfast, Mr. Montaigne. That is, of course, if you don't mind. Heaven forbid that I should disturb you. I realize that you value your time highly—or is it only that you can't find anyone to endure your company?"

She had done it again, she thought unhappily, and she felt like biting her tongue once the sarcastic retort had been released. This morning she had had no intention of insulting him, regardless of his needling. But the words were out, and she had no choice in the matter now. She gave him a half-apologetic smile and waited for the nasty reply she was sure would follow.

A smile lit Damon's strong features. "Ah, Alex, never can I remember being graced at breakfast with such charming company. Of course you won't disturb me." The smile broadened. "At least you rattle before you strike."

Even though she had expected the barb, it caused a pained look to cloud her eyes. "I'll just tell Letti what I want," she said quickly, rushing from the room.

She pushed past the swinging door to the kitchen and stepped inside on trembling legs. Inhaling sharply, she clutched her stomach, closed her eyes, and leaned against the wall.

"Heaven help us, child!" Letti exclaimed, hovering so close to Alex that Alex jumped when she opened her eyes. "What's wrong with you?"

Alex flashed her a hasty smile. "Oh, nothing, Letti. I guess I was still dozing a little. It's early for me."

"Don't I know it? Do you have some special plans for the morning that got you up so early?"

"No. I couldn't sleep. Maybe it was the excitement of the play last night."

"Hrumph! The excitement of the play. You poor little thing—you were kind of like the magnolia blossom that fell on the thorny rosebush, weren't you? Damon sure was mad at you. Why, I'd sooner turn loose a baby rabbit with a bunch of snakes than watch you in that triangle."

Alex winced at the metaphor. She particularly loathed snakes, and she'd already heard reference to them twice in the space of three minutes. And besides, she asked herself, what was so unusual about Damon being angry with her? "Really, Letti, it was a nice evening, and Casaundra, Damon, and Brent were very good company. I'm not a child, you know."

Letti's face creased into a smile. "And I'm not a spring chicken that can easily be fooled. What can I get you for breakfast?"

"I'll just have juice and toast this morning, thank you."

"Juice and toast! That's not a decent breakfast. You let me fix you some bacon and eggs, Alex."

Alex suppressed a denial. It did sound good after all, and she needed all her strength to parry Damon. "Fine, Letti."

When she went back to the dining room, Damon had lit a pipe and started to read the paper. Alex was happy that she would be ignored while she ate breakfast. At least when Damon was reading the paper, she felt sure that he wouldn't bother with her. But this morning she was wrong. Without laying the paper down or looking up, he puffed on his pipe, removed it from his mouth, and asked her through swirls of blue smoke, "Where are your cowboy boots, Alex?"

Her anger was instant. She would never forget his nasty remark about her boots the first time she saw him, and she hadn't worn them since. "Why?" she snapped. "Do you want to wear them?"

Laying down the paper, Damon looked at her almost fondly. "You *are* a little devil, aren't you?"

She refused to be baited again, choosing instead to look down at the silverware in front of her.

After a few seconds' pause, he spoke again. "I thought we might saddle Brownie and Stranger and tour the grounds this morning."

"Oh, could we?" Alex burst out enthusiastically, forgetting that it was impossible for Damon to be civil.

"Of course, if you think you can stay on a real horse."

"I can stay on a real horse," she retorted crossly. "I rode the horse trails several times in California."

"Oh, did you now?" he asked flippantly. "Well, I'll see for myself. You're probably used to broken-down nags. These are spirited animals here at Willowstone—a rare and special breed."

Letti came into the dining room with Alex's breakfast before Alex could think of anything with which to counter Damon's remarks. And besides, she reminded herself, she *was* used to broken-down trail horses. As much as she hated to admit it, she had told herself often enough that the poor horses she rode had seen better days. Without looking at Damon again, she stabbed viciously at her eggs with her fork, thinking to herself that she despised Damon enough to jab at him instead.

Walking self-consciously on the pavement in her noisy cowboy boots, Alex accompanied Damon to George Willis's house with mounting excitement. As angry as Damon made her, she still had high hopes that this riding excursion would be fun. Damon rapped sharply on George's door, and the small man appeared immediately, dressed in a dark red robe and house slippers.

"Yes, Mr. Montaigne?" He was obviously embarrassed at being caught in his nightclothes.

"Saddle Brownie and Stranger for us, will you, George?" Damon requested.

"I'll just be a minute," George murmured apologetically. "I didn't know you wanted to ride today."

"We didn't know it ourselves until a little while ago," Damon replied pleasantly. His kindness toward his help seemed to be entirely out of character, and Alex was surprised by it.

While George dressed, Damon and Alex walked out to the white-fenced pasture, and Damon whistled for the horses that were running together in the distance. With a thunder of hooves, the black stallion galloped over to the fence, exhaling steam in the early morning air as he stopped abruptly near Damon.

"How are you, Stranger, ol' boy?" Damon murmured affectionately, stroking the stallion's long neck.

Alex watched Damon with interest; it was the first time she had seen his gentleness.

"Isn't he a beauty?"

"Yes, he is," Alex agreed. "What kind of horse did you say he is?"

"A Spanish-Barb."

"I've never heard of them," she confessed.

"Most people haven't, though they have an ancient heritage. Spanish-Barbs originated in Persia, but under Moorish command they entered Spain and became the foundation for the famous Spanish horses of the fourteenth and fifteenth centuries. Later the American Indians, cowboys, and frontiersmen rode them. They almost became extinct when the large crossbreds came into favor. Fortunately, there were a few people around who realized their worth."

"Are their dispositions anything like their name?" Alex asked.

"No, they're reliable and intelligent. But they do have one peculiar trait—they tend to keep to themselves when pastured with other horses." He laughed. "I like a horse that prefers its own company."

He would, Alex thought, and she could understand why Damon preferred the snorting black stallion. The two of them shared some of the same characteristics; they were both wild, haughty, aloof, and barely civilized.

George saddled Stranger quickly, but the bay mare, Brownie, had to be coaxed into the stable with a bucket of grain. She was pawing at the hard ground to unearth a few green shoots of buried grass, and apparently she was unwilling to leave one treat without the prospect of another one.

Damon climbed easily into the saddle, but Alex realized ruefully that she was used to having someone hold the reins while she mounted. She struggled to straddle the horse when George handed her the reins, and she colored brightly when she saw the knowing look in Damon's eyes. George, seeing her predicament, looked quickly at Damon, then assisted Alex onto the mare's back.

Stepping about restlessly, the horse seemed to sense that she carried an inexperienced rider, and Alex nervously clamped her legs tighter around the horse's middle. Suddenly, the bay plunged forward, almost throwing the unsteady Alex over her head as she did so. Damon's mocking laughter was loud behind her as he pulled Stranger skillfully up alongside Brownie and halted them both.

"That, Miss Hawthorne," he taunted, "is a real horse."

If Alex hadn't been astride the animal, she would have walked away, but in her position she had to sit and endure his barbs. He had selected the right breed, she thought bitterly. A barb-tongued demon and a wild Spanish-Barb horse—an excellent combination!

"Well, now," he said, nettling, "would you like me to teach you the correct way to ride a horse?"

"I know how to ride a horse, Damon," she shot back at him. "You deliberately had this wild animal saddled for me. Nothing I did made her plunge forward."

"My dear Alex, you have wrongly accused me," he said, pretending that her words had hurt him. "You poked the toes of your boots into Brownie's sides when you clamped down with your legs. These animals are easily handled, but you can't blame the poor horse for your lack of finesse. Now, would you like some pointers, or are you still unwilling to admit that you know very little on the subject?"

Indignation surged through Alex. "Yes, Mr. Montaigne, by all means, show me whatever you want. That's why you invited me to ride with you, isn't it? You wanted another chance to humiliate me, didn't you?"

"Indeed not. As I recall, you told me you could ride, Alex." The words were almost gentle.

She glared at him with icy blue eyes but said nothing as he climbed down from his mount and stood by hers. Unexpectedly, he reached up and, putting his hands around her waist, lifted her from the horse. The softness of her body brushed against the hard length of his as he moved her to the ground much too slowly. Alex felt a quickening of her pulse and a throbbing inside her as she slid along his body and looked tremulously into his strangely glowing eyes. She truly hated him as she had never hated another man, but at the same time, her body cried out for his touch. She felt her lips quiver in expectation of his demanding kiss, and she wondered if he felt her excitement and the desire that raged in her at his very touch.

Her feet reached the ground, shattering any illusions she had held about him making love to her. Releasing her abruptly, he turned his head deliberately and began to point out the correct way to mount a horse. Though Alex went through the motions, following his directions precisely, she could think of nothing else but the breathless way she had felt as her willing body touched his. And she hated herself for her thoughts. She didn't even like the man, so how could she tingle so at his touch? She had come here despising him for what he had done to her father, but now she was reluctant to even mention the bitter topic. What had gotten into her?

Correctly mounted, Damon and Alex left the fenced enclosure to ride through the grounds. They followed a trail much of the way, saying very little as they viewed the hills and trees. White pines, lebanon cedars, cypresses, and magnolias stood alongside the barren limbs of huge oaks and maples. Leaves rustled softly beneath the horses' feet, and an occasional broken branch snapped, often sending some furry creature scurrying for cover. Several small brown deer, drinking from the little stream that meandered about the estate, fled quickly when Damon and Alex approached. Alex gasped at the beauty of their lithe bodies suddenly lifting in the air as they escaped.

As enthralled as she was with the wonder of the forest, she had to fight the distracting memory of Damon lifting her down from her horse. Her body persisted in defying her by wishing Damon would stop for some reason so that she could feel his hands around her as she moved against him to the ground, but they continued to ride through the woods without pausing. Damon occasionally commented on some particular aspect of the journey, pointing out the beauty of a red bird or the home of an animal as they passed, and once he thought he saw a fox, but Alex missed it.

When they reached an especially wide-open space, Damon told her, "You go on down the trail slowly, Alex, but I'm going to give Stranger a good workout. I'll meet you in a few minutes."

"Let me come with you," she urged. "I'm used to Brownie now, and I'm sure she could use a workout, too."

"No. You don't ride well enough, and you're too inexperienced with Brownie." With no further comment, he nudged Stranger, and the black stallion galloped away.

"You don't ride that well, and you're too inexperienced," Alex mimicked. Didn't he think she could do anything well? She had always considered herself quite capable, and she was sure she could manage Brownie now that she had ridden her awhile. Well, she would show Damon that she could ride as well as the next person. Though she was wise enough not to anger him by following directly behind, she waited only a few minutes before giving Brownie her head.

Brownie was off in a minute, pursuing Stranger at a rapid pace. Alex's breath caught in her throat at the sudden speed, and her heart did somersaults as the animal thundered through the woods, gaining speed at an incredible rate. The surging movements of the horse

frightened the wits out of Alex. She clung tightly to the
reins and tried to hang on to Brownie's sides without
poking her with her toes; she wanted to do nothing to
increase the speed of the lightning ride.

"Whoa, Brownie! Whoa, Brownie!" she cried, pulling frantically on the reins. "Brownie, whoa!" Much to
Alex's despair, her commands went unheeded. The
terrifying ride wasn't her only problem; the prospect of
actually catching up with Damon loomed large in her
mind, and it sent shudders to her very soul. "Stop it,
Brownie! Whoa!" she yelled.

But Brownie plunged on, dodging trees that reared
up out of nowhere. Alex felt the tears rush to her eyes.
It looked like her fate was pretty well sealed: she would
either be killed by Brownie or murdered by Damon.
No matter how fiercely she struggled to control the
headstrong animal, it dashed madly through the forest.
Alex felt her long blond hair whip wildly against her
shoulders and face. Her terror was rising. She had to
stop the horse! She had to!

With all her remaining strength, she grasped the
reins and pulled.

Miraculously, Brownie finally slowed to a halt. Alex
sat there stunned, trying to still her violently shaking
body, thankful that the horse had obeyed her at last.
She remained there berating herself for several minutes
before she urged the animal forward. Maybe Damon
did have a point about her being hard headed, she
admitted grudgingly. She'd just about gotten herself
killed on that darned horse. It seemed that she was bent
on confirming Damon's idea of her as incompetent and
willful.

Her breathing took several minutes to return to
normal. In the distance she saw the vague forms of
Damon and Stranger; she thanked heaven again for her
near escape. Nudging Brownie slightly, she encouraged
her to pick up her pace a bit.

With Stranger breathing hard, Damon reined in

alongside her. "Well," he remarked, looking thoughtfully at her, "this outing has been good for you. Your cheeks have high color."

"Yes," Alex managed to say. She was sure a lot more of her would have had high color if she hadn't finally been able to control Brownie.

All too soon for Alex, they had circled the property and were once again in sight of the stables. She was sorry to see them and sorry that the ride must come to an end. All in all, her little adventure notwithstanding, it had been marvelous. She was determined to thank Damon for showing her around, no matter what nasty remarks he made when they got off the horses. But fate was against her and she was to be robbed of the chance.

The sleek gold Cadillac was parked under the magnolia trees when they neared the house. Casaundra herself was leaning languidly against the white fence as they brought the horses to a halt.

"Oh, Damon," she called out petulantly, "you know I love to ride. Why didn't you phone me so I could ride with you this morning?" Her lips quivered a bit.

"Good morning, Casaundra," Damon responded cheerily. "I'm sorry. I forgot this is your morning off. Anyway, we didn't know ourselves that we would ride this morning. At the last minute I decided to show Alex the grounds."

"Oh, I wasn't aware that she could ride," Casaundra said.

"She can't." A twitching smile worked the corners of Damon's mouth. The remark caused an angry red flush to set off Alex's freckles. Damon moved easily from his horse, looping the reins around the fence post. "Well, come on, girl," he prompted Alex. "Are you going to sit there astride that animal all day?"

Stupidly, Alex realized that she had expected Damon to help her down as he had done earlier. She had deluded herself into thinking he had some manners after all, but she had been wrong—again. She tried to climb off the horse so fast that she almost fell on her face when one boot stuck stubbornly in the stirrup. "Darn!" she muttered.

"I see what you mean about her not being able to ride, Damon," Casauundra clucked, laughter touching her voice. Her eyes flashed with an especially vicious sense of victory.

Shaking his head at her ineptness, Damon freed Alex's boot, then waited for her to follow him through the gate. He pulled his pipe from his pocket and tamped the tobacco into the bowl while Alex looped Brownie's reins over the fence and caught up with him. She watched as Casaundra linked arms with Damon and began to chatter gaily. Alex dropped behind, tossing her head angrily. Let Casaundra be the one to feel Damon's touch, she thought bitterly. They deserved each other.

On the way to her room to freshen up, Alex indiscriminately yanked a book from the library shelves. Safely within the confines of her room, she soaked the morning dust off her body while she tried futilely to wash her thoughts free of the memory of Damon's searing touch. Oh, why was she letting herself get caught in his trap? Hadn't she learned anything from her father's dealings with the man? Damon wasn't trustworthy.

After she had gotten out of the tub and dried off, she slipped into the outfit she had decided to wear to the animal clinic. Then, trying to think of anything but Damon and Casaundra, she settled on the bed with Roadside to wile away the hours reading.

She was soon immersed in the book, which turned out to be about secret passages in old houses. Alex wondered if Willowstone had such a passage. The book said that the passageways had been especially common around the time of the Civil War.

The book proved so interesting that Alex didn't go down to lunch until almost two-thirty. She was relieved to find that Damon and Casaundra weren't around and she could enjoy her meal alone.

Deciding to leave early for Brent's clinic, anticipation finally overshadowing her morning excursion with Damon, she stepped into the burgundy Porsche. The car handled beautifully, and she smiled to herself as she maneuvered it skillfully along the narrow little streets of the old town. When she reached Brent's clinic, she parked and hurried inside.

Chapter Six

"I'm Alex Hawthorne," she told the receptionist. "I'll be working with Brent. But I guess he told you that."

"Ruth," the red-haired girl said, extending a hand. "Have a seat. He did tell me and he'll be with you in a moment."

Seating herself among the owners waiting with their animals, Alex looked around the simply decorated but neat and durable-looking room. When Brent entered, his eyes lit up, and Alex could tell that he saw her as an attractive woman, not at all as the headstrong, flighty girl who needed someone to make her decisions for her that Damon saw. "Ah, you're early. Good. Come on back."

Alex walked with him into the back room, where he handed her a gray smock and hung her coat on the hook on the door. "Let me give you a quick tour. We'll examine our first patient in five minutes."

Alex went with him eagerly. This was going to be her life's work. This was the reason her mother had made her promise to live with Damon, and this was the reason she had defied Damon's plans for her. She wanted to learn everything she possibly could from Brent. Besides, she told herself, if she became a success through Damon's contacts and money, she would in some small way be settling her father's score with him.

Brent showed her around the examining room, separated into two sections by a cloth partition. Off the main section was the x-ray room, with an elaborate x-ray machine like the one she had seen in her own doctor's office. In another large room were individual cages with cats, dogs, and birds in them. Off the x-ray room were two small surgery rooms. Brent explained how the anesthesia was given and how the animal was monitored during surgery, much as any human patient was. Beyond there was another large compound with runs for patients healing from operations. By the time Brent had shown her the flea dip and a device that looked like a big, old-fashioned stove used for drying the animals, it was time for the first patient.

Alex was so fascinated by the animals and Brent's expertise that she couldn't believe that four hours had passed when Brent looked up from examining the last patient. Reluctantly, she saw that seven-thirty had arrived. "Thanks so much for giving me the job," she told Brent earnestly as she shed her smock. "You can't possibly know how much it means to me."

"I think I can understand, Alex. I'm glad to be the one to help you." He smiled at her, and Alex felt his gaze travel easily over the length of her red sweater and multicolored slacks. Admiration was plain in the look, and she didn't know how to react to it.

"Let's celebrate your first day on the new job and the beginning of a long career in veterinary medicine for you," he suggested, his bright eyes glowing. "We can get a sandwich at the Fox Den and enjoy a few dances. What do you say?"

Alex didn't know how to answer. She didn't know if she wanted to become personally involved with him or not, or if she should, but she was grateful to him for all he had done for her, and perhaps he was only being kind. After all, he was Damon's friend. And she could sure use some kindness after living in a house with Damon. She smiled. "I'd like that."

When he slipped out of his smock, Alex permitted her eyes to skim his slender, wiry body, clad in a jumpsuit. He certainly had nothing of Damon's overwhelmingly masculine force, she thought to herself. But he was nicer than Damon—much nicer—and she was foolish to think so much of Damon's brand of dark good looks.

"Let me quickly check the animals, and we'll leave Ruth to lock up," he said.

Watching him, Alex wondered if she was making a mistake by encouraging his attentions. Too many times she had heard that office and play didn't mix, but she couldn't refuse him. Besides, she had enjoyed his company at the play. He was certainly different from Damon.

Before they left, Alex called Willowstone to leave the message that she was going out with Brent and would be late getting home. She despised herself for hoping that Damon would pick up, but Letti answered.

Alex noticed Ruth's half-concealed look of surprise when she and Brent started out the door. "Please lock up," he instructed. "I'll see you tomorrow morning." Suddenly, he snapped his fingers. "Just a minute. Let me get some books on veterinary medicine for you, Alex. I think you'll find them interesting."

When he returned, he handed her three thick books and opened the door for her to exit. She felt the pressure of his hand on the small of her back as they walked around the animal clinic to the rear, where his house was situated. "We'll drive my car. Yours will be safe parked here."

Alex hadn't had a carefree evening since her mother's illness had intensified, and she found herself becoming excited as they drove toward the nightspot.

The darkened room they entered was shaped like a cave, and it was much larger on the inside than the outside led one to believe. Featuring the rust colors of the fox, it was charmingly decorated with numerous pictures of the sly little animal. Glancing around at the nicely dressed people, Alex began to feel out of place in her casual clothes.

"I should have gone home and changed," she murmured to Brent.

"Nonsense. You look wonderful," he replied, his eyes searching hers intently. "Don't you know that you're the prettiest girl here?"

His sweet flattery pleased her. She could never imagine Damon saying something like that to her.

The words and music of a slow ballad flowed across the room, putting Alex into a dreamy mood as she sat down across from Brent at a small, intimate table.

"They serve coffee, soft drinks, beer, and sandwiches here. How about coffee and a sandwich? You're such a little thing, no one would ever believe you're old enough for a beer anyway," Brent teased.

"Sounds fine." Alex couldn't help but notice how gentle his teasing was, so different from Damon and his devilish taunts. She was glad Brent had invited her; she was beginning to relax and unwind after her exciting day. He moved to the counter to order their meal.

When he returned, a slow mellow song was enticing couples to blend silently together on the dance floor. Setting down the beverages and sandwiches and holding out his hands to her, he asked, "How about it? Would you like to dance?"

She stood up and melted into his arms. She and Brent, both with slender builds and fair coloring, made an attractive couple. As they twirled about the floor together to the slow throb of the music, Alex felt as if she had known him for a long time. He was easygoing, earthy and approachable—not at all like the supercilious Mr. Montaigne. Darn! she silently cursed herself. Why couldn't she just forget Damon?

Brent was murmuring something in her ear, and she

was shocked to realize that she had been so busy thinking of Damon that she hadn't even heard him. "I'm sorry. What did you say?" she asked softly, looking up into his face.

His mouth moved warmly against her ear. "I said you feel wonderful in my arms, as if you belong there."

Her lips curved into a smile. He was nice, really very nice. But when she closed her eyes and moved with him to the music, large hands were holding her, and dark eyes were looking into hers in the shadows of her mind.

When they returned to the table, Alex couldn't stop herself from asking, "How long have you known Damon?"

Brent shook his head as if he had been asked that question too many times. "I saw him about town most of my life, but I never really knew him until I went to work for old Doc Badger when I was eighteen. He and I went out to Damon's house to check on his horses. Surprisingly, he's almost compulsive about his horses—calls a vet at the slightest hint of trouble." He shook his head again. "Damon and I became friends when he found out I was a chess player. He has three passions—horses, chess, and women. And not necessarily in that order." Alex couldn't help but think that Brent sounded bitter as he spoke of Damon. There was a puzzling aspect to their friendship, but she hadn't been given any clues to it. Almost hesitantly, she began to question Brent.

"How good a friend is Damon to you?"

Brent looked pensive for a moment, and Alex thought she saw anger in his expression. "I already told you that Damon financed the office for me when I got my license. I could have taken over old Doc Badger's office when he retired, but the place was in pretty sad shape."

Alex sighed wistfully. "Is Damon as hard to get to know as he seems?"

Brent laughed softly. "The great, impressive Damon

Montaigne. Friend to the fortunate. Enemy to the unfortunate. Indestructible Damon. I have to give it to him. He's battled fiercely for everything he has, and he's come out on top." Abruptly, Brent stood up. "Excuse me. I need a beer. Can I get you something else to drink?"

Alex shook her head and watched him walk away. She felt that she was on the verge of gaining some useful information, and she waited tensely for his return. In less than a minute, he was back.

"How did Damon come out on top?" she prompted, trying not to sound too curious.

"The family clothing business was almost bankrupt when Damon's father died and he took over. At the same time, the secretarial school your father and he had started was hovering on the edge of failure. To make matters worse, your father left the city suddenly." Brent took a drink of the beer and looked away from Alex. "Your father really put Damon on the spot when he demanded to be paid for his share of the business. Yeah, people in this town said Damon was doomed to fail, but he proved them wrong. He worked night and day, and he made a success of both projects." He took another long swig of the beer.

Alex stared at him. "I don't believe my father left Damon in the lurch," she said defensively. "That's probably just the tale Damon told. Did you know my father?"

Brent suddenly seemed to tire of the conversation. "Let's say I knew him to see him," he admitted. "Hey, how about another dance?"

Alex put a hand on Brent's arm. "Let's talk," she coaxed, desperately wanting to stay with the subject. "Did it ever occur to you that Damon had lied about the business?"

Brent chuckled bitterly. "Lying isn't one of Damon's negative traits."

"If my father did what you say, why is Damon trying so hard to take an interest in my future? I refuse to believe that he's doing it out of the goodness of his heart."

Alex didn't feel comfortable with the frown that darkened Brent's face. "As hard as Damon is, and as hard as your father's leaving at that particular time was on him, he's still a man with his own code. He's never forgotten—and he doesn't let anyone else forget—that he owes his success to your father." Brent laughed harshly. "His code might seem odd at times—darned odd—but he never wavers from it. He's a man who demands respect and gets it."

He demands respect and gets it because he rides roughshod over people until they bow down to him, Alex thought resentfully. "My father wasn't the kind of man to leave another man in a bind without a reason," Alex stated.

"Who said he didn't have a reason?" Brent asked before taking a long drink of beer.

Alex felt her heartbeats quicken. Her breathing became shallow. "What was his reason? Do you know?"

Brent looked sheepish and shook his head. "None of my business. Come on. It's getting late, and I have to get up early tomorrow." Standing up, he held out his hand to her.

Very disappointed, Alex took it. She was sure she had been close to some answers this time, and again she was frustrated in her attempts to get them. Would no one tell her the reason for her father and Damon's feud?

When they got back to the Porsche, Alex didn't know whether to be glad or despairing when Brent kissed her lightly on her small nose.

"Be careful going home. I'll see you tomorrow morning. Good night, my beauty."

She whispered good night and climbed into the car. Her day had been full, and when she arrived home, she hurried into the house. Letti was waiting up for her.

"I've got hot chocolate waiting to be heated, child. I want to hear all about your first day at work."

Walking with her to the kitchen, Alex couldn't resist asking, "Where's Damon. Is he home?"

"No. Damon's gone. He left for New York this evening."

"Oh." Alex turned her head so that Letti wouldn't see the tears forming. He'd left again without telling her goodbye. Instead of hating him as she should, she found that she was terribly disappointed.

The next morning Alex reached the animal clinic promptly at nine. Ruth smiled at her as she hurried into the waiting room, still empty of patients. "Good morning," the redhead said. She turned knowing green eyes to Alex. "How was your evening last night?"

"Oh, it was very nice, thank you."

"It looked it."

"Oh?" Alex's eyes widened. "Did you see us?"

"Yes, I stopped by the Fox Den after I left the office, and surprise—there the two of you were, as cozy as could be, on the dance floor."

"You should have come over and sat with us," Alex offered, feeling slightly embarrassed at being seen to be so cozy with Brent so soon.

"I wouldn't have dreamed of disturbing you. I'm just so glad to see the doctor interested in someone besides Casaundra Calahan. He's carried the torch for her all of these years! It's high time he concentrated on somebody new; he's much too nice for her."

Alex felt the color drain from her face. Even though she'd thought Casaundra seemed possessive of Brent, she never imagined, never suspected that they . . . She sat down in a nearby chair and sighed.

"Oh, I'm sorry," Ruth murmured. "I didn't mean to be talking out of school. I just assumed that you knew about the triangle, considering that you live with Damon. Casaundra and Brent were high school sweethearts. Gee, I thought you knew. 'Course, I doubt that it ever really meant anything to Casaundra, but—" Abruptly, her words broke off, and her eyes moved to the file in front of her.

"Well, good morning. I didn't realize you'd come in." Brent's full attention was focused on Alex as his eyes scanned her bright yellow ribbed sweater and the golden pants that hugged her curves. "My, but you look bright and beautiful today. Come on back. I have two surgeries scheduled this morning before we see patients."

Spirits suddenly dampened because she couldn't seem to get away from the men Casaundra laid claim to, Alex walked into the back room.

Brent shut the door and stepped behind her to place a hand on her waist. "I thought about you last night when I should have been sleeping," he murmured.

Giving him a nervous smile, Alex quickly averted her eyes to the smock on the door. As she reached for it, she stepped away from him. "I'm ready," she announced unnecessarily as she slipped into the smock.

Brent took a towel from a glass-doored cupboard and laid it down on the table in the surgery room. Reaching into a cage, he removed a cloth-bagged cat and carried it to the table.

"Why is he in that bag?" Alex was amused by the sight.

"Have you ever been attacked by a nervous cat?" Brent asked, flashing her one of his boyish grins.

Recalling the evening Roadside had climbed across Casaundra and ruined her own stockings, Alex couldn't suppress a laugh. "Yes, and it's an experience I don't want to repeat."

She watched, fascinated, as Brent prepared the animal for surgery. Then she leaned forward as Brent worked; she didn't want to miss a thing.

As she watched, Alex had to fight a sudden dizzy feeling. She looked at Brent, and he seemed to be drifting away from her. Colorful stars danced and darted before her eyes, and she was aware of a ringing in her ears. *Alex, get control of yourself!* she ordered. *Snap out of it!* Becoming a vet entailed surgery and she wanted to become a vet. She forced herself to turn her eyes in the direction of Brent's skillful hands, but she felt a fluttering in her stomach, and someone seemed to have turned out all the lights.

"It's my first surgery," she murmured foolishly through dry lips as Brent looked up apprehensively from his work. Her eyes didn't want to focus, but she forced them down again to his hands. The hands seemed to become larger before her eyes, and she heard Brent call out to Ruth.

The floating sensation Alex felt was infinitely more pleasant than the terrible agony she had tried to endure as she watched Brent work. It was so peaceful where she was. Feathers and clouds drifted softly about, and she thought she heard a man gently call her name. His voice was low and soothing, and she thought she felt his light touch on her cheek. She searched for him, looking for dark smoldering eyes as her name grew louder in her ears. Her blue eyes fluttered open and she was startled to look into other blue eyes. In her confusion, her eyes darted around the room. For some silly reason, she had expected to see Damon, but she was stretched out on the waiting room couch, and the strong smell of ammonia stung her nostrils. Perched on the couch by her, Brent's eyes clouded with concern as he caressed her cheek.

Swift heat flooded Alex's body as the realization of what had happened dawned on her. "Oh, no!" she cried. "I didn't faint!"

"Out cold." Brent's smile was sympathetic. "I've been worried about you. You should have warned me. I was in the middle of surgery and couldn't do a thing to help you. I'm afraid you hit the floor before Ruth could reach you. Do you feel all right?" He began to gingerly explore her arms and shoulders, and she struggled to sit up before the examination progressed.

Her lips trembled. "I'm so sorry. I'm really fine. Is—is the cat all right?"

"Harry's just fine. He's in his cage now."

Alex tried to stand, but Brent eased her back down on the couch.

"Really," she insisted, "I'm okay—just embarrassed. I don't know what to say. I—I didn't have any idea that I would do that. Oh, how embarrassing."

"Hey, it's all right. I understand. The first time you see surgery is always the toughest. I just didn't consider the possibility of you fainting. It's my fault."

It was so typical of Brent, Alex thought, to take the blame for her stupidity. "Can I see the cat?" she asked, wanting to do anything to forget that she had literally fallen on her face during her first surgery.

"Are you sure you feel all right?" he asked anxiously. "Don't you think it would be better if you rested a bit longer? Let me get you a glass of water."

"No. No, really, I'm fine. Honest, I am. I'd like to see the cat." She just didn't understand it, she told herself as Brent put an arm around her waist to help her up. She was a person who generally took things in stride, but since her arrival in Danville, she seemed destined to create scenes designed to make her look incompetent. She smiled sheepishly at Ruth as she passed the girl to go into the back room with Brent.

The little cat was in a brown paper bag, and Alex wondered if he really was all right. "Why did you put him back in a bag?" she asked.

"For warmth." Brent lifted the little animal from the

bag; it was already coming out of anesthesia, its eyes glazed.

When the phone rang, Alex was grateful for the distraction. She didn't even want to talk about the surgery.

"Doctor," Ruth said, coming through the doorway, "Mr. Perkerton has a sick cow, and he needs you."

"Tell him I'll be over there in about fifteen minutes, Ruth." Brent turned to Alex. "Why don't you take the afternoon off?"

"What about the patients coming into the office?" she asked.

"They expect emergencies and they take them in stride. They'll wait, or come back later. In a small, mixed practice like this they know that anything can come up but Ruth can always reach me if something serious happens here."

Alex removed her smock quickly and slid into her blue jacket to walk out with Brent. She couldn't keep the unhappiness from showing on her face; her enthusiasm was thoroughly dampened, and she was depressed that her dreams had been shattered so soon. It had only taken her one day to realize now naive and ill informed she had been in her ambition to become a vet. What was it Damon had said—desire alone wasn't enough? How would she ever face him?

As she walked with Brent to a four-wheel-drive vehicle loaded with equipment, he wrapped an arm about her shoulders. "You'll get used to it. Don't look so down."

Alex didn't say anything, but she knew she would never get used to it. She raised big blue eyes to Brent. "You—you won't tell Damon about my day, will you?" she questioned tentatively. She could just picture Damon's "I told you so" sneer.

Brent hugged her to him. "What goes on between you and me is strictly our business."

Alex smiled gratefully at him. His compassion and understanding were limitless, and he never condemned her. Why, oh, why couldn't Damon have just a bit of this man's kindness? She kicked angrily at a pebble in her path. Why did she always have to think of Damon?

Alex's days in the animal clinic began to become routine, although she still couldn't watch a surgery. It meant the end of her intention to become a veterinarian, she realized ruefully, but she didn't tell a soul about her doubts concerning her future. She was too embarrassed to discuss it after she'd been so adamant. She continued to talk eagerly about the veterinary medicine field, and she read all of the literature Brent offered her. In secret, however, she found her eyes straying more and more to her history books, and those were the facts that filled her mind as the days without Damon passed.

She took an interest in the Civil War, and she began to read about the battles that pitted brother against brother over the slavery and states' rights issues. The bitterly fought battles and harshly contested skirmishes had destroyed thousands of lives and left the South dotted with graves and memorials.

The more she read the history books, the less she wanted to read the veterinary medicine books, and she dreaded the time when Damon would sit down to discuss her career with her. How could she admit she'd been wrong after she'd been so vehement about it? She couldn't bear to see his smug face when she told him she'd changed her mind. She'd rather die than admit he had been right. If only she hadn't been so sure about it. She sighed wearily; she was safe for now anyway. He was still in New York and the household was strangely quiet and empty without him. Roadside was free to roam the premises at his pleasure, though the library door was always closed to him.

At Alex's request, Letti was teaching her to cook the rich Southern foods that she had come to love, and she spent much of her time in the kitchen.

"You're a real good little cook," Letti told her after she'd helped prepare an especially delicious meal one night. "Wait till Damon comes home. He'll be real surprised."

Alex felt her heart jump. She didn't want Damon to know. "Oh, Letti, let's not tell him yet."

"But why on earth not?"

"I—I—let's wait until I can cook an entire Southern menu that will impress him. Then it will be a real surprise." She didn't want Letti to know she was sure Damon would find something wrong with her cooking, and she loved cooking too much to have him mock it.

When Letti answered the phone after dinner and exclaimed, "Why Damon, it's good to hear from you," Alex foolishly hung about the room pretending she was busy. But the truth was she hoped that Damon would want to speak to her. Of course, it was an absurd thought and very stupid of her to wish it. Damon didn't mention her name, let alone ask for her. After all, why should he? They barely tolerated each other, and really, she preferred it that way. Besides, she had Brent. He was plainly interested in her, and he was much more agreeable than Damon.

Alex began to see more of Brent socially. She had developed a deep respect for him, and she wondered why he had ever wanted a woman like Casaundra. They seemed so mismatched. When she got the chance, she wanted to ask Ruth more about their ill-fated romance, but she didn't want Ruth to know how interested she was in the triangle. Perhaps Ruth could shed some light on Damon's connections with her father, too.

Brent invited Alex to a Valentine's Day dance, and she decided she wanted a new dress for the occasion. When she told Letti about the dance, Letti agreed that it was quite a big to-do, and she would certainly need a new dress for it. All week Alex and Letti shopped, but it was the day of the dance before they found anything that Alex liked. The last dress she tried on was a long gown of clinging silk in a deep rose shade; it had a vee-necked bodice, cape sleeves, and a slight slit up the skirt front.

When Alex moved, the slit showed a hint of leg that somehow looked very daring beneath the molded fabric, which reached sleekly to the floor. The gown was beautiful, and Alex had her heart set on it until she fingered the price tag. Realizing it was much too expensive for her, she sighed wistfully and began to slip out of it.

"This is the one, isn't it?" Letti asked, smiling broadly, black eyes aglow. "Child, you look simply beautiful! Why, the first crocus of spring isn't any prettier than you are in that gown."

Poor Letti. Alex was sure she was tired of shopping, and she hated to tell her this couldn't be the dress. "I'm afraid not, Letti," she sighed. "It's much too expensive."

"Now don't you worry about the money. It's too beautiful for you not to buy it."

"Oh, it is lovely," Alex agreed, staring at the gown, "but I'll just have to look for something less expensive."

"No. No, you won't, child. I'll charge it. If you insist, you can pay me back later, but you really ought to have this one."

Smiling fondly at the old woman, Alex murmured, "Oh, Letti, you're just worn out from shopping, aren't you?"

"Indeed I'm not. I've got more energy than an old workhorse. I really believe you ought to have this dress. It's just made for you."

Alex turned to the triple mirror and pulled the gown back over her shoulders. It really was stunning. She did want it. "Well, perhaps I could get it," she conceded. "I can pay you with the money I earn working for Brent."

Letti's eyes danced with a bright sparkle. "Don't you worry about it. All that's important now is that you look beautiful. There'll be a lot of real rich folks at the dance. It's held every year in the Thorton mansion, and I'll want to hear all about it. Rumor is that the Thortons are heirs of Northern people—carpetbaggers who took over the plantation after the Civil War."

Alex shook her head in wonder. It was incredible to her that after more than one hundred years, these Southerners still strongly felt the division between North and South. But she had to admit to herself that she loved the history and the tradition the area was steeped in, and here in the heart of it, she found herself thinking as Letti did.

"How about these shoes?" Letti asked, holding up a high-heeled red shoe with an exposed toe.

Alex loved the shoes, and she selected a small elegant red clutch bag to complement them. With her prizes in hand, she and Letti hurried home to a quick dinner. Then Alex spent two hours dressing; she was dazzlingly beautiful when Brent arrived.

Again she had her blond hair piled high on her head, but this time it was a mass of bright silky curls from which two tendrils of shimmering hair like spun gold escaped behind one ear. She had accented her eyelids with a hint of rose and dabbed just a touch of pink on her already glowing cheeks.

When she entered the living room and set her white coat across a chair, Brent turned from the fireplace and whistled long and low. "My, my," he murmured huskily, "you look spectacular! Absolutely ravishing."

Blushing prettily, Alex let her eyes rove over him as he set down his drink and moved toward her. Dressed in a richly detailed suit of brown velvet, a lilac blossomed shirt shimmering across his wiry chest,

Brent looked suave and handsome. A lavender tie matched the lilac blossoms of his shirt perfectly. His golden hair and fair looks were highlighted by the dark color of his suit, and never had Alex seen him look so handsome. His face broke into a wide smile, revealing his even white teeth as he took a small box from his pocket.

"This is for you," he said, his voice low and mellow. Opening the box, he removed a delicate, gold necklace on which a very tiny sea gull, with wings spread, dangled daintily. She felt breathless as he moved closer to her and slipped the necklace around the exposed white column of her throat. She felt the movements of his hands on her neck as he fastened the clasp. They moved down her back to settle on her small waist, and he pulled her firmly against his chest. She was very much aware that he was attracted to her as his breath moved against her ear. "May your dreams ever soar," he whispered huskily.

Alarmed, Alex realized that he would be really hurt when he found out that she thought of him only as a friend. And she did, she now saw in a flash, care for him very much, but only in that way. Feeling a frantic urge to be free, she stepped out of his hands to peer into the massive mirror above the mantel.

"Oh, Brent," she murmured shakily, "it's so beautiful. You shouldn't have. Really, you shouldn't have."

She heard his quick steps behind her as he wrapped his arms around her waist. "Nothing is too much trouble for you."

"Shouldn't we be going, Brent? Won't we be late for the dance?" She couldn't help but note the high pitch of her voice.

His light laughter broke the electrified atmosphere. "Sure, honey. Sure, we should be going." Releasing her, he picked up the white coat she had placed on the chair and helped her into it.

Chapter Seven

They drove to Richmond, a distance of a hundred and fifty miles, for the dance. When Alex looked about the historic city, she recalled reading that it had been the true capital of the Confederacy during the four years of the Civil War. Eagerly, she questioned Brent about local monuments, but to her disappointment he confessed to knowing nothing about the history of the town.

The mansion they stopped in front of was even more magnificent than Willowstone. A uniformed young man hurried out to assist Alex from the car before taking the keys from Brent to park it. An aloof butler, clad in gleaming black and white, answered the doorbell. Alex and Brent were formally led into a massive ballroom whimsically and romantically decorated with ivory cupids and rows of valentine hearts in glittering pink. A buffet of delicious miniature sandwiches, bits of ham and cheese, trays of shrimp, and a host of other delicacies, was laid out on a lace-covered table of vast length. Roses and red carnations were situated at strategic points among the fancy dishes. Several cut-glass punch bowls with exquisitely designed cups nestled on the lace cloth. Alex's eyes widened as the butler directed them to a full-size bar.

"Enjoy the party," he said, as if it were possible that they wouldn't.

"The lady will have sherry," Brent told the bartender, "and I'll have a bourbon on the rocks."

Alex's head turned to take in the gorgeous room. She decided that its owner must surely be fabulously wealthy and that its history must be very impressive. The house was probably older than Willowstone. She looked up at the intricately patterned ceiling, which supported several teardrop chandeliers. Everything in the room seemed to require her immediate attention.

Though she received several admiring glances herself, she seemed impervious to them, so busy were her eyes. She felt as if one of her history books had opened its pages to admit her, and she didn't want to miss a single item.

She marveled at the fancy-gowned ladies and the elaborately dressed gentlemen twirling easily about the floor. Her attention was caught by the music coming from the end of the enormous room, and she was astonished to see a full orchestra. She glanced from couple to couple as they whirled gaily about the glistening marble of the dance floor.

"Alex," Brent said, breaking into her musings. Taking her arm, he directed her to one of the small tables bordering the dance area. Admiring the beautiful rose-and-carnation centerpiece, her hand reached out to cup a petal before she sat down on a red velvet chair that seemed designed to go with her gown and shoes. The tiny sea gull rocked gently against her throat with her movements.

For some time she and Brent sipped their drinks in silence, enjoying the atmosphere and the sounds of the beautiful music. When a lovely, old-fashioned waltz began, Brent stood up and held out his hand to her. "Shall we?"

She moved into his arms. She was aware that he pulled her just a little too tightly to his chest, but she was too entranced with her surroundings to protest. She wanted nothing to spoil the moment. It was almost like a dream to Alex as she floated about the floor with the handsome, blond Brent smiling into her face. They were in perfect step as he spun her smoothly around the room.

Alex was shocked when a dark, handsome, devilish face appeared behind Brent's fair one. Losing her step, she stumbled clumsily against Brent, and he pulled her supportively closer.

"May I cut in?" The deep voice was insolent in its mockery.

Staring at the man with faint annoyance in his eyes, Brent conceded a grudging yes.

"I thought you were in New York!" Alex sputtered, the hand Brent had released flying to her cheek. As Damon pulled her to him, the slow waltz gave way to a faster-paced love song. Alex was so stunned that she moved clumsily as Damon danced her across the floor in a fury. She remained upright only because he held her so tightly. He never slowed his step or acknowledged her discomfort, and Alex had the uneasy feeling that he meant to punish her for some unknown transgression.

"I *was* in New York, Alex," he said at length, "but I never intended to stay forever." A strange smile tugged at the corners of his full mouth. "Why? Did you miss me?"

The question caught her off guard, and she trembled slightly in his arms. Oh, why did he tease her so? Was it impossible for him to be nice to her?

"Well?" he persisted impatiently, bending his head nearer to hers so that she saw the mocking glint in his dark eyes.

"Of course not!" she retorted.

The devilish eyes studied hers for a brief moment; her eyes wavered under the scrutiny. "Obviously," he murmured, his voice dangerously deep as he held her tighter against his broad chest. "I didn't expect to find you at home pining for me—but neither did I expect to find you here plastered to Brent's body."

"And I didn't expect to find you here at all," she snapped, irritated by his unceasing gibes. Flaming blue eyes met mocking brown ones.

"What?" he exclaimed with pretended surprise, heavy brows meeting. "Why, my dear Alex, this dance is the social highlight of the year. Casaundra wouldn't have missed it for anything."

Again Alex stumbled against him, the movement crushing her breasts to the soft material of his suit. Why did her heart jump when he mentioned Casaundra? Of course, she should have known he would be there with her. How could she have been so stupid not to have thought of it? Her eyes instinctively searched the room for the woman, but she was whirled about so furiously that she couldn't focus. She missed another step and looked up into Damon's smoldering eyes. Why was he so angry? She couldn't bear his bold gaze and her eyes lowered to the expensive cut of his burgundy suit.

"Do you need dancing lessons, or is it me?" he taunted. She could feel his gaze on her face.

"Oh, I'm sure it's not you," she flared. "You do everything so well, don't you? Well, I was doing beautifully myself—with Brent. If you'll just excuse me, I'll go back to him." She turned to free herself from his grasp, but his large hand closed more tightly around hers, imprisoning it as he jerked her to him so fiercely that the tiny sea gull danced against her throat. She was almost smothered by his nearness as he looked down at the ornament. He permitted his lazy gaze to fall to her rapidly rising and falling breasts.

"Don't be in such a hurry," he drawled. "I'll struggle through until the music ends."

Legs threatening to crumple beneath her, she had no

choice but to struggle through, too, until the song was over. Never did she remember a song lasting so long or a torment so thrilling.

Damon relaxed his grip slightly, and she managed to move more gracefully with him, but she was painfully aware of his closeness. His very body heat seemed to set her on fire. He kept his smoldering eyes on her every moment, and she was almost hypnotized by his look.

"I like your dress," he offered, unexpectedly. Foolishly, Alex smiled brightly at him. He had never given her a compliment before.

"I'm glad I got my money's worth, even if you did wear it for Brent," he continued in a flat voice.

"Your money?" she rasped. "*Your* money?"

"Yes, Letti told me she put it on my account."

Alex felt the color deepen in her cheeks. "She—I—you're horrible!" she hissed at him. "Horrible!"

"And you're only a naive girl flaunting a woman's body. What are you doing here with Brent?"

"I suppose the same thing you're doing here with Casaundra!" Naive, he had called her! Just who did he think he was? She was woman enough for Brent.

"The same thing?" His eyebrows rose slightly. "Really? You shock me, Alex!" He grabbed her elbow as the music ended and guided her back to a table where Brent sat with Casaundra. Brent hadn't seen them approach, and Alex was surprised to see how close he was sitting to the woman and how earnestly he was talking to her. Alex's heart dropped at the sight of Casaundra, in a long gown of crimson silk that accented her darkly dramatic looks.

"Stay and join us," Damon told Brent, ignoring the daggers flashing in Casaundra's dangerous dark eyes. Alex thought the woman looked positively threatening.

"We wouldn't dream of breaking in on your party," Brent said, disregarding the fact that Damon had ordered, rather than invited, them to stay. "Would we,

Alex? We have our own table, and we'll just stroll back to it."

Certain that she couldn't endure another evening in the company of Casaundra and Damon, Alex smiled gratefully at Brent. Her eyes met Damon's with a triumphant glitter, only to be cast down at the unveiled displeasure she saw there.

Without another word, he sat down and began a conversation with Casaundra. It was plain that Alex and Brent had been dismissed. Unruffled, Brent rose from his chair, put his arm possessively about Alex's waist, and led her back to their table.

But the wonder and the magnificence of the evening had suddenly vanished for Alex. She wished she hadn't come to the dance with Brent. And wished even more that Damon hadn't come with Casaundra.

Somehow the evening wore on. Alex went through the motions of having a good time, dancing, chattering with the ever charming Brent, returning his smiles and beaming at his compliments, but her heart was as lifeless as one of the empty valentines suspended about the room. Whenever she saw Damon and Casaundra, both tall and darkly · handsome, whirling beautifully about the dance floor as if fate had decreed that they were made for each other, she turned her head away. She tried not to see the way Casaundra openly laughed into Damon's handsome face or the way his hands held the exotic woman so possessively.

When Brent suggested that they leave, since they had such a long drive back, Alex was more than willing. Once in the car, she laid her head against the car seat and closed her eyes in relief. But to her disgust, all she could see was Damon's devilish face. And all she could think about was the way she had felt in his arms. She was still thinking of him when Brent took her hand and escorted her to Willowstone's wide porch.

Wanting to be polite, she murmured, "It was wonderful, Brent—more wonderful than anything I ever imagined." And it would have been the truth. The evening would have been wonderful—if Damon hadn't shown up.

In the light of the full moon, Alex saw Brent smiling. "I'm glad you enjoyed it, Alex." Unbuttoning her coat, he slid his hand around her waist and pulled her to him. Tilting her head back, he lowered his head until his lips met hers. Her heart beat wildly against his chest, and she could almost hear his heart answering the beat, but as she sank deeper into the depths of the kiss, she realized it was Damon she was thinking of. She actually imagined that she could hear his steps on the walk— those heavy, ominous steps that had pursued her before.

Then he spoke!

"I beg your pardon," the deep voice bit out sarcastically. Guiltily, Alex jerked herself free of Brent's arms.

"Home early, aren't you?" Brent asked with annoyed deliberation. "You must have left immediately after we did."

"Oh?" Damon drawled. "I didn't notice."

I'll just bet you didn't, Alex wanted to say. But she couldn't. She didn't understand it, but somehow Damon had the power to make her feel ashamed of kissing Brent. She thought she would scream if she stayed there in the company of the two of them a minute longer. "Good night, Brent," she whispered raggedly. Without looking at Damon, she opened the door and disappeared inside.

Alex slept late the next morning, strangely uninterested in rising from her bed at all. The memory of Brent's kiss came again to her mind, and hovering behind it was Damon's face as it had looked when he suddenly appeared behind Brent at the dance and again at Willowstone's front door. The man was contemptible, she thought, feeling herself flush anew at his treatment of her. And yet—and yet she couldn't escape her visions of him. Even worse, she had but to open her door and go downstairs and she would be forced to confront him. He was the most abominable, cruel, insensitive, exasperating individual she had ever encountered in her entire life. Nothing in her twenty years had prepared her for this man, yet his was the touch her body yearned for, his was the kiss her lips called for, and his burning hands were the ones that seared her flesh with their tiniest touch. At his nearness, even her loyalty to her father's memory vanished. Brent's kiss had been nice, his arms had felt good around her, but the arrogant, antagonistic Damon was the man who remained like a fire blazing in her mind.

It was ridiculous! She turned over and pounded her pillow with a fist, glad that it was Thursday and she wouldn't have to face the day at all if she didn't want to. She remained in bed, tossing sleeplessly, until Roadside jumped down to the floor and began to prance about restlessly, mewing with ever louder insistency. She knew he was hungry, and he was not in the habit of being kept waiting for his breakfast. Pulling on her pink chenille robe, she picked up the smoky kitten to take him downstairs.

Slipping silently past the closed library door in her furry slippers, she padded down the hall to the dining room. She entered with the gently purring Roadside, half expecting to find Damon reading his morning paper, but the room was empty. She pushed against the swinging door to find Letti at the kitchen table reading the newspaper with a big cup of steaming coffee in one hand.

"Morning," she called out cheerily to the small, slightly disheveled girl. Alex hadn't been able to brush out last night's coiffure, and her hair turned up in an unruly mass of blond curls. "That must have been some Valentine shindig for you to sleep so late. I wanted to ask you about it last night, but I was so tired before you got home, I just couldn't wait up." She got up from the table. "I'll get your breakfast."

With a firm hand, Alex motioned her back to the chair. "No. No, Letti. You sit down and finish your coffee. I'm not very hungry anyway. I just want to feed Roadside. Then I'll get something light—orange juice and a roll, I think. Didn't I smell fresh-baked sweet-bread when I came in last night?"

Letti hopped up from her seat again. "You sure did, child. Fresh-baked walnut bread. I used black walnuts from our own trees. I'll heat you a big slice with some butter. I got some fresh-made butter from the Sparks's farm last evening, and it's rich and delicious."

Alex put her hand on the woman's shoulder. "Sit down. I'll manage myself, after I feed Roadside. Read your paper."

Looking a little bit hurt because Alex wouldn't allow her to perform her duties, Letti sank reluctantly back onto the chair. "The breakfast is my responsibility, but if you insist, you can get your own. Then come back here and tell me about the dance. I'm just dying to hear all about it. Mrs. Sparks's granddaughter went with some boy from out of town. She's a pretty little thing, but I'm willing to bet that you were the belle of the ball."

Alex tilted her head and slanted her eyes at Letti. "In Damon's dress."

The housekeeper looked guiltily at the floor for just a moment before she raised her head defiantly. "And why not? Damon can well afford it, and he wants to get nice things for you."

"Oh, does he now?" Alex retorted. "Oh, Letti, why didn't you tell me you were charging that dress to Damon's account? I never would have let you do it."

Letti's eyes glinted mischievously. "And don't I know it? That's exactly why I didn't tell you. I wanted you to have that dress, and I know what a stubborn little bit of baggage you are, child. My, my, but you do take after your daddy. I just knew you'd get all independent if I told you it was Damon's account. I don't have a charge account in that store." Her smile was wide. "I sometimes pick up things for Damon there, but that's the most expensive store in the whole county."

"Well, I'd take the dress back today if I hadn't already worn it!" Alex's blue eyes narrowed. "I don't want to spend Damon's hard-earned money on such trifles, let me tell you."

"Why not, Alex? Damon wants to do for you. Why must you be so mule-headed about his generosity, honey?"

"Because—because—" The words tapered off and Alex threw up her hands in despair. There was no way she could explain to this woman how she felt about Damon. After all, Letti had practically raised him herself. She couldn't tell her how rude and impossible and overbearing and stormy she found him to be, how ruthless and taunting and—and how exciting and enticing he was to her. And, of course, she couldn't tell the woman how she wanted to hate him for what he'd done to her father.

"Damon was real fond of your parents, Alex. They spent a lot of time together. They knew each other for years. Your grandmother Hawthorne worked in the Montaigne clothing store. Damon's friendship with your family was a deep and abiding one. You're wrong not letting him take care of you." Letti looked at Alex with solemn eyes, but it was apparent that her suggestion hadn't made a favorable impression on the girl who stood silently stroking the kitten.

The old woman shook her head, causing the single gray plait that hung down her back to dance. "I'm sorry if you feel that I'm speaking out of turn, child, but Damon is the nearest thing to a son I'm ever going to have, and I've become real fond of you, too. It seems a real shame to me that the two of you keep on knocking heads. For the life of me, I can't understand it. Neither of you has any family, and I remember how delighted Damon was when he told me you were coming to live here. He wanted to do something to make up for the chance your father gave him when they started the school together. Damon didn't know anything about running a school, but he had a determination that was missing in your father. He saw that a school that focused only on business classes was useful, and he forced your father's dream to work long after Allen gave up, turned tail, and took you and your mother to California."

Yes, Alex thought bitterly, long after my gentle, sensitive father gave up his dream, Damon pushed on like a relentless machine to achieve his goals, rob my father of his idea, and cheat him out of his productive years. "Why, Letti? Why *did* my father go to California? I know he didn't just run out on Damon. What did they quarrel about?"

For the first time, Letti looked as if she wished she hadn't started the conversation. "You were such a child when your father left, Alex. You were too young to know how people can get messed up through their own weaknesses. Your father couldn't hold up under the pressure of starting a business. He—he needed excuses for his failings—he—"

"He what, Letti?" Alex prompted. She was tired of hearing insinuations and slurs against her father's character.

"He thought your mother was being unfaithful to him, and he wanted to leave Danville."

There! Someone had finally said it, thought Alex, but she was too shocked to absorb the information. She couldn't believe it! It couldn't be true! Suddenly, Roadside spat at Alex and gave an ominous hissing cry. Alex, welcoming the distraction, murmured, "I'd bet-

ter feed this animal before he gives up and does
something drastic." Shaking the kitten's furry head
playfully, she tried to suppress the depressing revelation that Letti had just let slip. She wondered briefly if
all the ugly rumors could be true. Had her parents
really been the people she had believed them to be all
her life? Or had she simply failed to recognize their
weaknesses? And what did all this have to do with
Damon? It made her heart ache to think such
things . . .

Forcing a smile, she opened a can of cat food for
Roadside and scooped the contents into his dish. After
freshening his water, she went to the refrigerator for
the orange juice and the fresh butter Letti had mentioned. Slicing off a big piece of the delicious-looking
walnut bread, she popped it into the modern micro-
wave oven cleverly concealed in the colonial kitchen
wall. A tantalizing aroma teased her nostrils as she
waited the scant half minute it took the bread to heat.
Her breakfast in hand, she opened the door for
Roadside to scamper outside after his hastily gobbled
meal. Then she took her breakfast to the big wooden
table where Letti was reading the paper.

The housekeeper looked up as Alex sat down. "Well,
child," she said with determined cheerfulness, "are you
going to keep me in suspense all day? Tell me about the
dance. I've heard about the Thorton mansion, of
course, and I've seen the outside a couple of times, but
I've never been in it. What was it like?"

Alex was ready for light conversation. "Oh, Letti, it
was too beautiful for words—even lovelier than Willowstone."

"Pshaw!" Letti grunted, refusing to admit such a
possibility.

"It really was! A butler answered the door and led us
to an actual ballroom decorated with ivory cupids and
big pink valentine hearts. There was a live orchestra

and a fancy buffet. Real roses and red carnations were used as centerpieces. Where would the Thortons get those flowers this time of the year?"

"Most likely hot-house flowers that they paid a fortune for," Letti mused.

"Oh, you should have seen the mansion. It was like something out of a book. There—"

The kitchen door swung open. "Good morning, Letti. Alex." Damon's voice was thick and lazy as if he, too, had just gotten out of bed. He cast a decidedly cool glance in Alex's direction. "I trust you enjoyed the party last night. You certainly seemed to be having a good time clinging tenaciously to Brent."

Alex looked down at her orange juice and resisted the temptation to throw the wet, sticky contents into Damon's smug face. "Thank you," she countered icily. "I enjoyed myself tremendously—especially before you and Miss Calahan arrived."

"Miss Calahan!" he repeated. "Well, aren't we formal? And is it also Dr. Haggerman?"

Alex stared mutinously at him. "It most certainly is not."

"No, I didn't think it would be, the way he was smothering you at the front door," he snapped dryly. "Letti, how about two eggs and some grits. I'll also have a large slice of that walnut bread, that is"—he looked down at the big piece on Alex's plate—"if Miss Hawthorne hasn't taken it all."

Picking up her plate, Alex slammed it viciously down on the table near where Damon stood. "Here, take this one!"

She rose swiftly and started to stalk away. The sleeve of her robe brushed across the plate, sending it clattering to the floor. "Oh!" she cried furiously. Humiliated, she looked down briefly, seeing the broken blue willow plate and the smashed bread on the floor. With flaming cheeks, she kicked at the mess and stormed out of the room. She heard Damon's mocking laughter as the swinging door continued to move back and forth behind her.

Her pride in shreds, tears streamed down her bright, hot cheeks as she marched up to her room, stripped off her nightclothes, and ran a tub of hot water. Stepping into the soothing waters, she tried to let her temper simmer down, but she had absolutely no luck. That man was infuriating! He was an absolute monster! Why on earth was he able to get her goat all the time? It only frustrated her to the point of making a fool of herself.

As she fumed, she remembered what Letti had said about her parents. She didn't believe a word of it! Either Letti was mistaken, or Damon was behind the lies. She was beginning to wish she had never asked about the rift between the two men. The more she heard, the worse the story sounded. Why, oh, why had her mother wanted her to come here?

It was some time before she emerged from her room dressed in silver-gray slacks and a pink sweater. Since she had finished the book on secret passages, she picked it up to return it to the library. But when she came to the foot of the stairs, the telltale odor of tobacco smoke caused her to head past the library door. She would wait to replace the book until he was gone. Instead she went outside to retrieve Roadside.

A bitter, cold wind was blowing under a cloudy sky. For a moment, Alex looked up to watch the billowing clouds chase each other across the lowering sky before she searched for the kitten. She didn't see him anywhere, and it was unusual for him to stray. Hugging her arms to her body, her teeth chattering with cold, she hurried around the yard, calling to him, coaxing him to come, but he wasn't to be found. By the time she went back inside, she was shaking from the cold. She dashed madly through the house, briskly rubbing her chilled arms as she looked for Roadside.

"Letti, have you seen Roadside?" she asked, seeing the housekeeper stacking dishes in the dishwasher.

"Might find him with Damon."

"Damon?" Alex's voice was incredulous. Turning quickly, she hurried across to the library. Damon was sitting before a massive wooden chess set, idly toying with the men. To her total disbelief, Roadside was chasing a brightly colored sash that Damon was dragging across the floor with his free hand.

Recovering her voice, Alex asked, "Did you let Roadside in?"

"I did," Damon replied lazily without bothering to look up from the chessboard.

"Why did you do that? Do you intend to let him break something else in this room so you can add it to my bill?"

Damon looked up, dark eyes flashing fire. "Indeed I do not! Two such fiascos are enough!" He looked back down to move a chessman before he allowed his eyes to roam up her body from her small loafered feet to her wayward golden hair. "I've grown rather accustomed to the little charmer, and occasionally I enjoy his company." Waiting for the words to sink in, he added, "Don't look so surprised, Alex. I do have needs and desires somewhat akin to those of other human beings."

Alex looked at the taunting face, waiting for the next gibe, but it didn't come. In fact, Damon appeared to give her an honest smile, and she simply stared at him. She had nothing to say.

"Having established that shocking fact," he said, "is your chess game any better than your riding and your dancing, Alex?"

"No, Damon. Actually, it's decidedly worse," she replied tartly, "so I'll just take my kitten and leave you to your own company. I'm sure it will be much more enjoyable—and much more accomplished—than mine." She reached down to pick up Roadside, who insisted on holding on to the sash, catching it up in his claws and pulling obstinately on his end while Damon clung to the other. Alex glared at him before yanking the sash free of the kitten's grasp. Then she hurried from the room. She had reached her own room before she realized that she had forgotten to put the book away. She tossed it angrily down on her desk, fighting all the while against a ridiculous urge to cry.

Chapter Eight

Alex cooled down as the hours stretched into a typical winter day. Damon was away from the house much of the afternoon, and she spent her time browsing in the city library, where she checked out several books on chess. She'd be darned if Damon Montaigne was going to get the best of her in everything.

When she returned home, she took the book on secret passages downstairs to replace it. She was just reaching up to put the book on the shelf when Damon came up behind her. She gasped in surprise; she hadn't known he was in the room.

Ignoring her fright, he said, "I see you've been reading about secret passages, Alex. Letti must have told you about the one in this house."

Alex's interest was immediate. "No. Is there one here?"

"Then Letti didn't tell you? Yes, we have one here. I'm quite intrigued by it. When I had the house remodeled, I kept it as a conversation piece. I was told that the original owner had a fear of being caught in his own home without a means of escape in case of war, intrusion, or what-have-you. Would you like to see it?"

Alex felt giddy with anticipation. Of course she

wanted to see it, but she didn't want Damon to know how eager she was. "Yes, I would."

"It's here in the library—a rather clever setup," he said, removing some books from a shoulder-level shelf. "This knob frees a panel beside the book shelf. There's a rumor that during the Civil War a number of soldiers hid in the passage. I've tried to track down some facts on it, but I've only managed to run across people whose relatives have heard the story." He moved a barely visible knob and stepped over to a panel grooved like all the rest of the panels; it slid behind the others at Damon's touch.

"Are you interested in history?" she asked, astonished that they actually seemed to have something in common.

"Greatly."

She should have known, she told herself, when he told her the history of the Spanish-Barb horses.

She peered into the dark, eerie opening, and she could barely make out a ledge with some steps leading down into deeper darkness.

"I'll get a light if you feel like exploring," he offered, much to her delight.

"Oh, Damon, I'd love to. The passages I read about in the book sounded so fascinating."

Excitement mounting, she waited while he went for a flashlight.

"This way," he said when he returned. "And do be careful. It's very dark and it can be treacherous. No one has been through it in a long time." He stepped through the opening and she followed, trying to keep him in sight. "Hold on to my shoulder going down the steps," he instructed. "They're old and weak."

Obediently, Alex put her hand on his shoulder as she moved down the steps behind him. It was very spooky, and she felt the goose bumps rise along her arms and neck. She was intensely aware of the packed dirt walls of the tunnel, shored up by heavy wood beams. The single beam of light in Damon's hand did little to keep the blackness at bay.

When they reached the last step, she let go of his shoulder. "Where does the tunnel come out?" she whispered. Just as she spoke, she felt something brush across her face, and she had to cover her mouth with her hand in order to stifle a scream.

"What's wrong?" he asked, his voice concerned. "Are you afraid?"

"No. No, of course not," she denied, her heart hammering. She was terrified, but she wouldn't admit it. "Something—there was something that brushed across my face."

"Probably spider webs," he explained, and she shuddered at the thought.

"I asked where the tunnel leads," she said in a louder voice, trying to muster some courage.

"It comes out in the stable. It really is quite ingenious. One could simply climb on a horse and flee."

"It is ingenious," she agreed, beginning to feel chilled as they went deeper into the tunnel. The farther they went, the muskier it smelled and the damper the walls became. Alex began to wish she had thought to wear a coat.

As Damon flashed the light off to one side, Alex thought she heard something move. Were there mice down here? Or even rats? This time Alex was unable to stifle her scream or to stop herself from stumbling backward involuntarily.

Damon reached back and took her hand, drawing her a little closer to him in the process. She was somewhat relieved, but even his comforting presence couldn't still the frantic desire she felt to turn and run back to the safety of the library.

"It's all right," Damon murmured. "I thought you

were fearless and quite able to stand up to anything."

She gulped twice before she found her voice. "I—I was startled," she said in a low voice. "I thought I saw something move." Fearless? Her legs felt like rubber bands and her stomach had turned several somersaults in the last thirty seconds.

"You're shaking," he said, squeezing her hand. "You *are* afraid."

"No, I'm not," she insisted stubbornly, unwilling to admit her own weakness. "I—I'm cold."

"Oh, I'm sorry, Alex. Of course you are. I should have told you to wear a coat. I just assumed your sweater would be warm enough." He turned and wrapped his arm about her shoulders, hugging her to him, and she felt a dangerous excitement. Somehow that was more frightening than her fear of the tunnel, but nevertheless she put her arm around his waist and clung to him as they made their way through the rest of the tunnel. Finally, she forced herself to stop shaking— at least, outwardly—but her insides quivered uncontrollably. She couldn't understand why his nearness inflamed her senses so intensely. She was so caught up in the sensations his closeness caused in her that she forgot about the damp, chilling darkness all around her.

Eventually, he stepped in front of her and, taking her by the hand, started up some steps. Although she was still inside the tunnel, Alex could see that they were nearing the end; the blackness had given way to dull gray. Damon pulled a lever, and Alex was surprised to find that they were in an extended wall inside the barn. Boards parted automatically and they slipped through a narrow opening into the comparative brightness of the stable. The horses whinnied softly, and Alex looked around in wonder. Damon was still holding her hand, and she felt a sudden coldness when he released it to show her how cleverly concealed the secret panel was. He moved the panel back in place and it blended in with all the other boards, which were adorned with an assortment of stable paraphernalia.

"It's very interesting," she agreed, realizing that she appreciated it much more now that she was safely out of it. Besides, she couldn't seem to concentrate on it with Damon standing so near. "Thank you for showing it to me," she murmured, staring up into his eyes. It was ridiculous, but she had the strangest yearning for him to take her in his arms and kiss her.

He stared down into her eyes, and she shivered with anticipation. "You're cold," he said, pulling her against his body and briskly rubbing her back. She was sure he was going to kiss her, but he turned away from her instead. "We'd better get back to the house."

She was cold, but only because he had taken his warmth away from her. She wanted to tell him to take her hand again or wrap her in his arms. She wanted to—but she walked with him back to the house in silence. When they returned to the library, he offered to explain the construction of the passage to her and she nodded eagerly. She didn't want him to leave her. He told her there was a similar tunnel described in the book. But as he reached up to take it from the shelf, the phone rang.

"Excuse me. I'll just be a moment. I'm expecting a call," he said.

He answered the phone with a pleasant hello, but when he turned to Alex his voice was suddenly biting. "It's for you. Don't tie up the line all afternoon. I'm waiting for a business call."

Feeling his fingers brush hotly against her own as she took the phone, she was very aware of his hostility. She sighed wearily. He certainly ran hot and cold. "Hello," she said, decidedly displeased that her caller had chosen such an inopportune moment.

It was Brent asking her if she had slept well and if she was thinking of him. She was embarrassed as he began to whisper sweetly to her while Damon stood in front of her, apparently with no intention of allowing her any privacy. She put her hand over the mouthpiece and whispered, "Do you mind if I have a few words with Brent alone?"

"I don't care if you fly to the moon with Brent," he growled.

In her irritation, she turned her back on Damon and said, "I'm sorry but I can't talk now. Damon is expecting a call. Perhaps you could ring me later. Goodbye."

Slamming the receiver down in its cradle as if it were responsible for her bad mood, she walked back to the secret passage. The panel was closed now, making it impossible to tell which section was movable, and Damon was gone. Alex shrugged her shoulders and walked to the den to switch on the television. Just what did it take to keep him from getting angry with her all the time? She might as well have kept talking with Brent, who was at least pleasant. Smiling to herself, she thought about the things he had said to her. He wasn't anything like the cruel, volatile, unpredictable Damon. She made up her mind to question Ruth about Brent's romance with Casaundra; she was curious about how deeply he had cared for the woman.

Hoping to catch Ruth before Brent came in for his afternoon patients, Alex left for the clinic early on Friday. However, when she arrived Brent was already in, propped up on Ruth's desk talking to her.

"Good afternoon," Alex said.

"Good afternoon," Ruth answered warmly.

Brent's eyes lit up. "Good afternoon, my beauty. You're early. Couldn't stay away from me, huh?" His face broke into a big grin, and Alex blushed as she looked at Ruth's plain, smiling face. "I'm sorry I didn't get a chance to call you back yesterday, but I got tied up. Did Damon get his call?"

"I don't know," Alex admitted, rubbing her arms briskly. She didn't want to talk about Damon. "It's so cold today, isn't it?"

"Looks like snow," Ruth remarked.

The bell rang, announcing the beginning of the regular flow of patients. "Work time. They're early, too," Brent said as he and Alex walked back to the examining room, where she put on her smock. While kneeling on the floor, after examining a cat in the lower cage, Brent watched her intently for a moment. When he stood up, he stole a hasty kiss. Alex couldn't hide her startled expression, and he laughed.

"What were you thinking, my beauty?"

She looked away from his eyes to the medicine-lined shelves. "I don't know," she lied; she had been thinking of Damon and how he had played with Roadside in the library.

"Did I tell you that you were the most beautiful girl at the Valentine's Day dance?" Brent murmured, putting his hands around her waist and pulling her to him. "I'm afraid you've stolen my heart away."

She laughed lightly, trying to cover her discomfort as she backed out of his arms. "You hardly know me."

"I know." He beamed wickedly, arching his brows with a mock-evil look. "I've got to rectify that. I want you to meet my parents, Alex."

Staring at him, she didn't know what to say. He reached out to draw her back to him, but the phone began to ring shrilly, shattering the tenseness of the moment. Alex was relieved when Ruth entered the room.

"Farm emergency, doctor—one of Mr. Anderson's pigs. I told him you would get over there as soon as you could."

Brent smiled. "Thanks, Ruth. Why don't you explain to the people waiting, put a sign on the door, and close up shop for the day. The weather looks bad and I don't know when I'll be back. You two take the day off. I'll see you tomorrow."

Alex watched as he removed his smock and hurried to the door. She waited until he was gone, then turned to Ruth. "Are you in a hurry to go someplace?"

Ruth shook her head. "Nope. I was planning to be here until eight tonight. Have you got something in mind?"

Alex smiled. "Well, actually I was hoping we'd get a chance to talk. Do you remember that conversation we started about Brent dating Casaundra before she became interested in Damon?"

The red-haired girl returned the smile. "Yes. I did rather leave that story in the middle when Doc came in, didn't I? Say, why don't you come to my place for coffee and a sandwich? I have some good roast beef."

It was just the opportunity that Alex had been waiting for. "I'd love to," she agreed.

With Alex driving behind Ruth, it only took ten minutes to get to the big old house where Ruth lived. The building had been converted into apartments and Ruth's was as cozy and homey as Alex had expected it to be. Ruth put some coffee on, and the two of them settled down for a pleasant talk.

"It seems as if things are getting pretty serious with you and Doc, judging from the way he looks at you," Ruth said, her eyes twinkling.

Alex laughed nervously. "I'm afraid he's moving way too fast for me."

"I guess he wants to be sure Damon doesn't take *you* away from him, too," Ruth said.

"Why, what do you mean?"

"Well, Casaundra dated Doc pretty steadily all the way through high school. Doc planned to marry her when he completed his vet studies—"

"He was that serious?" Alex interrupted in surprise.

"I think so. He was definitely crazy about her,

though I sure don't know why. They were inseparable until the day she begged to go with him to Damon's to play chess. She said she wanted to get a close look at Damon."

"And I guess Damon liked what he saw and just took over," Alex said with annoyance. It sounded just like him. For a moment she was tempted to ask more about Damon, but she pushed the thought aside. She was here to find out about Brent, she reminded herself.

"Oh, I don't really think it was a case of Damon taking over," Ruth mused. "I guess Damon and Casaundra were attracted to each other—she is beautiful—but actually it was your father who threw them together. Casaundra was young—about nineteen, I guess—and she'd just returned from a finishing school in Europe. She insisted that she wanted to put her newly acquired skills to use, and though Damon and Allen couldn't really afford a secretary, Allen thought that Casaundra's money and connections would attract wealthy young ladies to the school, so they hired her. The first thing this town knew, she and Damon were a twosome and Brent was the third wheel."

"But didn't Brent object?" Alex asked, incredulous.

"Oh, he objected, but Brent isn't much of a fighter. He was just gradually crowded out of the picture as a boyfriend, though he has continued to be friends with both of them through the years. Other people thought he never really cared that much for Casaundra, but I knew better. I went to school with him, and I know how badly he took it. He and I both used to work for old Doc Badger." She toyed with her watch. "But really it was the best thing that could have happened to Brent—getting rid of Casaundra. She's nothing but trouble." Ruth looked Alex squarely in the eyes. "For everybody."

For just a moment it occurred to Alex that Ruth was trying to warn her about Casaundra, but the idea was ridiculous, of course. Her imagination was always running away with her these days. She forced her thoughts back to Brent.

He sounded like a man with no backbone, she thought ruefully, but she brushed the thought from her mind. He was just kind, and she really did care for him. Besides, he would certainly be nicer to live with than Damon. Maybe she ought to try to think of him the way he so obviously wanted her to. For just a brief second, Alex thought about asking Ruth if she knew the story behind her father and Damon's rift, but she was too embarrassed. Each time she had learned something about the breakup, the story had gotten more shameful. She didn't have the heart to put herself or Ruth on the spot.

"Well, I'll get the coffee and make the sandwiches," Ruth said, getting up to go to the kitchen.

While Alex waited, she looked about the room and saw a small chessboard. "Do you play chess, Ruth?" she called out.

"Yes. Love the game."

In a few minutes, Ruth was back with the food. "I've even beaten your Mr. Montaigne." She was evidently very pleased about it.

"You're kidding!" Alex exclaimed. She couldn't believe her good fortune.

"Nope. I'm not kidding. I learned from old Doc Badger, who also taught Brent and Damon. We spent hours playing on winter days when business was slow. We kept a board in the old clinic."

"Have you beaten Damon often?" Alex asked eagerly.

"I can't say often," Ruth confessed, "but on occasion."

"Will you teach me to play?" Alex pleaded.

"Let's eat these sandwiches, and then I'll be glad to. I love the game almost as much as Damon does."

It was eight o'clock and very dark when Alex first thought about the time. She was sure Letti would be concerned about her if she didn't get home, and it was time she left anyway. She and Ruth had been so engrossed in their game that they hadn't even looked out the window to see that darkness had settled in. Alex had caught on to the game very quickly under Ruth's patient guidance, and she was surprised to find it so intriguing. She discovered that she had a natural ability for it; once she got her mental gears oiled and learned the moves, she was able to plan ahead far enough to capture Ruth's men. She hated to stop playing, but after they made plans to play one night each week, she got up to go home.

When she stepped out the door, she was thrilled to see thick snow pouring down in the beam of the street light. Suddenly a flood of memories of sled rides and gleeful children having snowball fights rushed to her mind. Elated to see the snow swirling about, she danced in the falling white flakes, happily waving her arms and catching bits of fluff with her hands. "Look, Ruth," she exclaimed gaily, "it's snowing!"

The other girl watched her antics with an indulgent eye before giving a cautionary suggestion. "Do be careful driving home, Alex. The snow is beautiful, but it's already sticking to the roads and it can be very dangerous."

"Oh, don't worry about me," Alex assured her. "I'll be fine. Nothing this beautiful can be harmful."

But Alex was wrong. Fifteen minutes later, on the isolated road to Willowstone, unable to see the lines hidden under a blanket of snow in the darkness, Alex felt the tires lose their grip. She had driven off the road; she heard a grinding crunch as the car slid sideways into a ditch!

For a moment she sat there with the engine idling, totally surprised and unsure of what to do. The accident had only stunned her; she wasn't hurt, she noted with relief. Looking about in dismay, thinking surely someone would come along and render assistance, she waited in the car. The minutes ticked by slowly and all that happened was that she used up a great deal of gas and got rather frightened in the snow-filled silence. If her situation hadn't been so pathetic, she would have laughed hysterically.

Mentally shaking herself, she finally attempted to open the car door, but to her horror she found that it was wedged against the gully's side and wouldn't budge. She was trapped! she thought wildly. Trapped in the snow! Oh, dear, what was she going to do now? It was several frantic seconds before she gathered her wits enough to slide to the passenger side, where she pushed the door open, and climbed out with great care. The snow wasn't very deep yet, but it was coming down with a vengeance, and the ground was soggy where the car had skidded off the road.

Slipping and sliding on the slick road, she walked around to the back of the car to stare with apprehension at the vehicle lying in the ditch. Studying the situation carefully, she decided that with enough power the car might pull free of the gully, so she slid back inside and put her foot firmly to the gas petal. Please, she prayed, let it work. The engine spun angrily and the tires whined, but to no avail. When she got out to check her progress, she found that the car had settled deeper into the snow.

"Darn!" she muttered helplessly. "Oh, darn!" Why hadn't she listened to Ruth? But she had been as careful as she knew how to be, driving in unfamiliar weather conditions. Now she was hopelessly stuck here, at least a mile from Willowstone and with no other houses in sight. She didn't know whether to remain in the car or start out on foot before it got even colder and the snow got deeper. Cursing her brown loafers, now wet with snow, she tugged harder at the too-thin blue jacket and stared nervously down the dark road in both directions. The only light was at the intersection some distance away. In the falling snow, it cast a shadowy glow across the road. Surely, she told herself, someone would travel down this road and see her predicament. But she really wasn't sure at all.

As she stood there uncertainly, shivers of fear crawled up her spine. It was awesome in the dark night with the snow-covered shadowy surroundings caught in the harsh glare of the car's headlights, and when she thought she heard a movement in the pasture beside her, she had to fight down a rising scream. It was probably just a cow. She was sorry now that she had dallied so long at Ruth's apartment just to learn chess so she could beat Damon. Even when he wasn't around, that man was a thorn in her side. And how would she ever tell him about his car? The thought of it was enough to make her shake harder than from the cold. What was she going to do?

"Darn!" she muttered again in frustration. This time she was really in trouble. She slid back into the car to turn off the engine, shut off the lights, and retrieve the key. She couldn't just stand there staring at the disabled car. She had to do something. She decided she might as well try walking. Surely it couldn't be very far to Willowstone. When she moved forward, she saw that the darkness in the absence of the headlights was almost complete. Stumbling back to the car, she fumbled around until she got the door open, then searched the glove compartment for a flashlight. Finding none, she rummaged desperately around the floorboard until she located a small one under the front seat.

Caught in a new moment of indecision, she didn't know whether to go or stay, but, pulling her jacket tighter around her, she set out determinedly on the lonely, snow-whitened road to Willowstone. Unused to the treachery of the snow she had so briefly considered beautiful, she slipped and slid along the snowy patch that she hoped was the road. She thought she could make out some half-concealed fencing along the edges of the road, and she kept flashing the light from one side to the other, trying to use the fencing as a guide. She stumbled often in her slippery loafers, and she gave an occasional gasp as she pitched forward unexpectedly. Snowy shapes seemed to loom out at her as she trudged wearily along, and more than once a scream ripped up her throat and had to be forced back down again. Never one to enjoy walking, she was tired in no time, and the added burden of trying to keep her footing in the snow made her wonder if she would be able to make it all the way. But she couldn't turn back now.

At one point she thought she heard the roar of a car engine, and she moved hastily off the main section of the road only to stumble into the gully alongside. Her foot lost its hold and she pitched forward on her face, burying herself in the soft snow. Furious, she stood up with some difficulty and staggered back up the incline, angrily brushing off the snow, only to find that the car had turned off before it reached her anyway. She felt tears of frustration and weariness start to her eyes. The snow she had fallen in had melted with the heat of her body, and her clothes became soggy, increasing the cold she felt. Not long afterward, she thought she heard the whine of an automobile again, but this time she was more cautious about getting off the road.

When she had stepped aside, hoping against hope that it was someone who would give her a lift to the mansion, she surprised herself by wondering if it was safe to accept a ride with a stranger—even under these conditions. Maybe she was better off to keep stumbling along the road? How much further could it be? She felt a mounting fear rise in her as she was caught suddenly in the glare of headlights. The car ground to a halt, and the driver, huge in the night darkness, jumped out and ran toward her. He looked menacing in the glare of the lights, and Alex gasped at the swiftness of his movements. She had no intention of permitting him to overpower her! Swinging the flashlight into position, she directed the beam right into the man's face.

Blinking and flinching angrily at the sudden glare, Damon put up a hand to shield his eyes. "What the devil are you doing?" he demanded through tightly clenched teeth. "Why are you walking? Have you had an accident?"

She was too weary to take offense at his anger. "Oh, Damon, I'm so glad to see you," she exclaimed, clutching at him with her cold hands, her body trembling.

He lifted her up in his arms, crushing her to the warmth of his chest. "You're soaking wet!" he exclaimed. "Are you hurt? Where have you been? The clinic closed hours ago. I phoned and I went by there when the snow started. Where's the car?" The staccato questions blasted at her, and it took her a moment to digest them. She looked up into his face, but his expression was unreadable. Without waiting for answers, he opened the car door and put her on the seat.

"Where's the car, Alex?" he repeated.

She should have known better than to think he was concerned about her, she thought tiredly. He was worried about his precious car, and he had decided something must have happened to it. Weary with physical and mental exhaustion, temper rising as fast as his anger, she snapped, "No, I'm not hurt in case you're really interested. And I'm just out for a brisk walk for my health!"

Harshly, he grabbed her shoulder and turned her to face him. "Where is the car?"

"Back down the road" she answered curtly. "Otherwise I wouldn't be strolling in this direction!"

"Is it all the way off the road?" he demanded.

"Yes, it's off the road!"

Carefully and skillfully, he pulled back onto the

road. "Then it won't do any harm to leave it there tonight."

"You don't have to worry about your precious car," she said tartly. "It isn't damaged—much," she added with just a degree of concern. "It slid into a gully."

Shoving the car into gear, he maneuvered it forward in the heavy snow while Alex huddled in her corner for the silent drive home. When Damon turned the heater control to hot, she leaned forward gratefully to meet the stream of warm air, but she couldn't help but think that he would never thaw out. If it was possible, his stony, angry face and his chilling silence made her even angrier than she already was. The evening had taken its toll on her nerves, and she was in no mood to endure his barbaric disposition.

As if matters weren't bad enough, she saw the dim shape of another vehicle in the driveway of Willow-stone when they approached. She didn't want to see a single soul tonight, and she hoped she would be able to flee to her room unnoticed. Without waiting for Damon, she jerked the car door open and headed toward the house. Flinging the front door open, she ran into the hall—right into Brent's arms.

"Alex," he murmured, concern clouding his face, "what happened?"

For just a moment she looked up into his eyes and saw herself reflected there. Her hair was wet and matted, her clothes damp, and her shoes squished when she walked. "Oh, Brent," she whispered, clinging to him as his arms tightened protectively around her. "Oh, Brent, the car slid off the road in the snow. I—I've never driven in the snow," she defended, "and—" Tears fell from her eyes and she began to sob, more from relief than for any other reason.

Lifting her head up to brush back a strand of wet hair, he asked anxiously, "Are you all right?"

"Yes, she's all right," a voice snapped from behind

them. "Go to your room, Alex. Get a hot bath and put on some dry things before you catch pneumonia."

"Now just a minute here," Brent intervened. "I want to know what this is all about."

"It's none of your business what it's about, Brent," Damon answered evenly. "You were invited here for dinner and a game of chess, not to watch over my houseguest."

"I'm not trying to watch over your houseguest, Damon," Brent retorted defiantly. "I happen to be in love with Alex, and I intend to marry her."

Alex was no less astonished by the revelation than was Damon, who looked at Brent in disbelief while Alex stared first at one of them, then the other. "You happen to what?" Damon asked.

"I happen to be in love with Alex," Brent replied with more control.

As angry now at Brent as she was at Damon, Alex thought that he might have discussed the question with her first. He would certainly be surprised to find out that she *didn't* love him!

A low chuckle bubbled up in Damon's throat, becoming a deep mocking laugh as it left his lips. "You must be snow-blind, Brent. You haven't known Alex long enough to be ready for such a serious involvement. And Alex certainly isn't ready for it." Dismissing the whole affair as a ridiculous joke, he shrugged, "Let's go have a drink. We could both use one. Alex, go and clean up!"

Anger was building in Alex like a brushfire. Pushed past the point of control, she bristled under his gaze and his words. She was too drained by her ordeal and too surprised by the evening's revelations to take any more of Damon's heavy-handed treatment. "I'll go when I'm good and ready. Don't think you can order me around just because I'm staying in your home. I'm quite capable of making my own decisions—about everything! My love life is none of your business—"

Anger stretched to the point of violence, Damon pointed a finger toward the steps. "Will you go—now?"

"No!" she shouted, balling her hands into fists. "No, I won't!"

She wasn't prepared for his sudden movement. In a flash he had hoisted her up under his arm and started up the steps, hauling her by his side in the crook of his arm like a sack of potatoes.

"Put me down!" she raged, kicking her feet furiously as she looked back at Brent with blazing eyes and a flushed face. "Brent!" she called frustratedly. "Brent!"

"Now see here, Damon," Brent protested, but Alex noted contemptuously that he didn't take a single step in her direction.

Damon marched right up to her room with her in tow, flung the door open, and plunked her down on her feet. "Now," he grated, "get in there, take a hot bath, and get on some dry, warm clothes."

"You—you monster, stop ordering me around!" she demanded, moving swiftly away from him. "Just who do you think you are? Get out of my room. You don't own me!"

Damon grabbed for her and ripped off her jacket. "Stop it!" she shrieked, flailing at him with her hands as he grasped the bottom of her sweater and yanked it upward. In seconds it was over her head and on the floor, and the clasp of her bra was unsnapped.

"Wait! Wait!" she rasped, grabbing at her bra with both hands. "Wait! I'll do it."

"Then see that you do," he insisted, giving her one last look before he turned on his heel and left her.

With trembling fingers and a pounding heart, she peeled off the rest of her clothes and hurried to the bath.

Chapter Nine

Shaking uncontrollably, Alex stepped into a tub full of hot water. She wasn't sure if she was shaking from cold or the chilling shock of the scene she had just endured. She was still reliving all of it in her mind when she slipped into the soothing waters and sighed. All she knew was that she never wanted to return to the two men downstairs. Soaking as long as she dared, she finally slipped into a robe and began to dry her hair with a portable dryer. She would have remained in her room longer, but she was startled by a tapping on her door. Fearing that it was Damon, she opened the door reluctantly.

She was very relieved to see Letti smiling at her. "I heard about the accident, child. How could I help but hear?" she mused distractedly, running a hand across her forehead. "Are you all right?"

"Oh, Letti," Alex breathed. "I thought you were Damon. You scared the wits right out of me. Yes, I'm all right."

"Well, then you'd better get dressed and come on downstairs. You'll feel better when you get some dinner in you."

"Honestly, I can't eat a thing."

"You need to eat, child. It'll make you feel better, and besides, Damon is—"

Alex finished the sentence for her. "Waiting dinner for me, and I know how he hates to be kept waiting at dinnertime." Didn't that man care about anyone else's feelings? she wondered wearily. Didn't he realize that she'd suffered through quite an ordeal tonight and was on her last legs, physically and mentally?

Letti smiled encouragingly at her. "You get dressed in something warm and come on down."

Forcing herself to pull on a pretty shamrock-colored dress, Alex stood surveying herself in the mirror. The dress was plain, but the sleeves were long and it was comfortable. Her appearance definitely improved, she felt better about facing Damon and Brent, and after she had slipped into some low-heeled shoes, she trailed down the stairs.

On entering the dining room, she was surprised to find Brent speaking companionably with Damon as if nothing at all had happened; it made her extremely curious about the exchange between the two of them that had occurred in her absence. Taking a chair next to Brent, she permitted her eyes to rest on him and he smiled at her with sympathy. "Feel better now?"

She returned the smile. "Yes, thank you, I do." Remembering that he had said he loved her in the hall, she fell silent for a moment, wondering where the conversation could go from there. Seeking a neutral topic, she said, "I didn't know you were coming to dinner tonight, Brent."

"I realized that when I saw you in the hall. I forgot to mention it today after the emergency came up. Damon had invited me earlier in the week, and I wasn't sure I would be able to come. He and I often share a meal and an evening of chess."

Alex stared at him in wonder. It wasn't at all obvious now that just a short time ago the two men had very nearly come to blows. She almost wondered if she had imagined it, but she couldn't forget Damon's hands against her flesh as he yanked off her sweater, and the thought of it caused her to blush. She had been strangely excited by his treatment of her.

"Oh," she murmured absently. "Is—is the animal all right?"

"Fine."

Alex turned away from Brent to glance at Damon, and he caught the look. He seemed to have been waiting for it. "Well, Alex, are you all right now?"

"Yes, of course," she replied crisply, looking away from him, her head held high. Soon Letti brought in the meal, and at the sight of the heaped platters Alex decided she was hungry after all.

Letti joined them for dinner, and her friendly chatter helped the meal pass quite pleasantly. After coffee and cherry pie, Damon and Brent retired to the library to play chess, and Alex was left to try to sort out her jumbled feelings. It was infuriating how Brent's ardor seemed to have cooled in her brief absence, though she certainly didn't know what she would have done if he had mentioned love again. She was sure Damon had had a hand in the matter.

Finally, amazed at how quickly she had ceased to be the topic of interest, she followed along to the library to watch the game. She didn't let on that she had learned to play herself. She was saving that surprise for Damon until she felt she was skilled enough to have a chance at beating him.

After several games, in which he was invariably the loser, Brent stood up and went to the front door to see how deep the snow was. Deciding he could drive home safely in his four-wheel-drive vehicle, he thanked Damon for dinner and the chess and beckoned to Alex.

Embarrassed, she joined him at the front door. She had felt Damon glaring at her when she walked away from the library, and somehow she felt terribly self-conscious standing in the hall with Brent.

"You get some rest tonight, and I'll see you at the clinic in the morning," Brent whispered, pulling her close. His mouth descended to hers, and he kissed her swiftly. Alex could think of nothing but Damon waiting in the library, knowing she was here being kissed by Brent, and she slid from his arms and stepped backward.

"Good night, Brent. Be careful of the road. I can testify that it's slippery out," she said with a nervous laugh. She wished she could forget about the snow. Indeed, she wished she could forget about the entire evening, but she knew she couldn't.

Placing his lips against her forehead, he murmured, "Good night, my beauty."

Without a word to Damon, Alex hurried up the steps to her room, where she quickly changed into her nightie and slipped into bed. After the evening she'd had, the bed felt like heaven, and, snuggled contentedly beneath the quilts, she was soon drifting into sleep.

A sharp rap on her door shattered her peace, jerking her fully awake.

She slid her feet into her furry slippers and went to open the door the scantiest bit. "Yes," she said, seeing Damon in the hall.

"You forgot to wish me good night, Alex," he drawled suggestively.

"Good night." Her voice was an angry hiss as she pushed at the door to close it. He reached out in an attempt to keep it open.

"No gratitude to me for rescuing you?" he asked mockingly.

"Thank you," she muttered crossly.

"That's not good enough. Open this door."

"Why?" she demanded.

"Because I told you to," he said calmly.

"It's late and I'm very tired."

"I want to talk to you," he insisted.

"Talk to me in the morning."

Suddenly he shoved the door open with such force that Alex was pushed backward. "I hate games, Alex. I said I want to talk to you and I intend to do so."

Backing away from him, she went to her bed, climbed on top of the covers, and hugged her pillow protectively against her nightie. Then she sat there staring at Damon with wide eyes.

"What do you want to talk about?" she asked in a tight voice.

"You. You, Alex," he replied dryly. "Nothing in my household has been the same since you arrived. Nothing. And now I find that you fancy yourself in love with Brent."

She hadn't said she fancied herself in love with Brent—she knew quite well that she wasn't—but she would never give him the satisfaction of telling him that. "I didn't ask to come here, Damon," she snapped crossly. "As a matter of fact, I didn't want to, if you remember. It was, I believe, your idea. And my mother's. It was my understanding that you had this burning desire to see to my education."

He laughed softly and the sound was strangely loud in the still room. When he began to walk toward her, she shifted her position uneasily.

"Little did I know, my girl, what a task I was taking on," he murmured, shaking his head as he eyed her peculiarly. "But I don't regret my part of the bargain. I want to see to your future, and I *will* see to it. What worries me now is your sudden interest in Brent. It might interfere with my plans for you, and I could never permit that. What brought it about so quickly?"

"That's none of your business," she retorted.

"I beg to differ. It *is* my business," he stated evenly. "I have your welfare at heart, and I don't believe you're in love with Brent."

"And what do you know about love, Damon?" she demanded.

He settled himself on the bed beside her, and she felt her breath catch in her throat at his nearness. "I know enough about love to know you aren't in love with Brent Haggerman," he responded easily.

"I doubt that," she snapped.

Suddenly the pillow was ripped away and she was in his strong arms. Pulling her across his lap, he crushed her to his chest. Alex felt a thrill rush through her. His head descended and his lips claimed hers, plundering, caressing, manipulating, teasing with a savagery and skill she had never experienced. He tangled his fingers in the hair at her neck and forced her lips to move against his own. Taken by surprise, she resisted fiercely, struggling to free herself, but she was hopelessly imprisoned, and each movement sent a new shock of pleasure dancing through her body. Sliding his hand down her back and then around to her breast, he cupped it gently, causing Alex to melt against him. Her hands reached up to tug possessively at his hair before they slid down his muscled back, pulling him nearer, ever nearer to her. Her lips parted beneath the onslaught of his and she feasted on his kiss, never wanting his mouth to leave hers.

Standing up with Alex held tightly in his arms, Damon turned and gently placed her on the bed. Alex watched in eager anticipation as he stretched his muscular form over hers and lowered himself to her. Her arms returned possessively to his back and she lifted her mouth to meet his. For a moment Damon stared at her with strange, brooding eyes. Then he rolled away from her and spoke huskily. "I told you that you weren't in love with Brent." Without another word, he rose and left the room.

"I hate you, Damon!" she cried after him. "I hate you!" But the door slammed shut and she was alone with her anger. Clenching her teeth in fury and humiliation, she slid under the covers, rolled on her side, and began to sob. He was right. She wasn't in love with Brent. She was in love with Damon. And it was sure to cost her her heart.

Alex stirred in her sleep. She was dreaming that lips as light as feathers were touching hers, gently nibbling with a tingling, tickling touch that teased her senses. The man in her dream looked like Damon, and she was pleased by his warm, knowing caress. She stretched languidly, a smile playing lazily on her lips. She opened her eyes and looked with disbelief at the man who stood beside her bed. With a start, she jolted wide awake.

"Damon! What are you doing here?" For a moment she imagined that she hadn't been dreaming at all. She thought that Damon had actually been kissing her. Shaking the ridiculous thought from her mind, she glared at him. "You've got some nerve! Don't you have any regard for a woman's privacy?"

A hint of a smile played across his lips. "This woman has to get up and help me locate a car."

"Oh," she mumbled. She had forgotten about the car she had left stuck in the snow last night. "But I have to work at the animal clinic today," she said hopefully.

"I called Brent and told him you wouldn't be in today."

"Oh, you did," she said. When he nodded, she realized that he was determined that she go with him. "I'll get dressed," she said, sighing.

His dark eyes roamed over her tousled hair, her large sleepy blue eyes, and her mouth with just a hint of last night's lipstick. Self-consciously, she dragged her fingers through her hair. "Well, do you want me to get dressed or not?"

His half-smile became full blown. "Suit yourself."

"Well, get out of here," she muttered, irritated that he played with her feelings so callously. Her eyes rested on his mouth and she shivered at the memory of his harsh kiss last night.

"I wonder, Alex," he mused, "if it were Brent standing here, would you be so quick to dismiss him?"

"Oh—you monster!" she hissed. "Get out of my room!" She raised a hand, intending to slap at him. As she moved, the covers slid from her upper body. The valley between her breasts showed in the vee of her nightgown, and Damon's eyes settled there brazenly. She grabbed at the covers and glared at him. "You have no manners at all!"

With an infuriating calm, he smiled at her, reached out to tweak her nose, and sauntered from the room.

Anger consuming her, she stormed from the bed. He was horrible! And this was the man she loved! A cruel, teasing, taunting, uncivilized heathen! She wished she had never met him. And she wished she had never driven his car. But more than anything she wished the darn thing wasn't stuck in a gully. Thinking of the snow, she pulled on jeans, a sweater, and her cowboy boots and took a deep breath in an attempt to control her anger. Just let Damon make a crack about her boots this morning. She'd let him have it with both barrels!

She marched down to the dining room table, ready to confront him, but he wasn't there. Sighing with frustration, she went to the kitchen, where Letti was frying country ham and green apples. "Oh, it smells delicious, Letti," she said, the thought of breakfast putting her in a better mood. She stepped up behind the housekeeper and peered over her shoulder.

Letti turned around, her nose a bright, angry red. "Oh, Alex, good morning," she mumbled, her voice altered by her stuffy nose. "I can't smell a thing. I've got a humdinger of a cold today. It's clinging to me like soot to a chimney."

"I'm sorry to hear that," Alex said sympathetically,

concern furrowing her brows. "You go on back upstairs
and I'll finish breakfast this morning. I'll bring a tray up
to you."

"No, child, thank you, but the breakfast is my job
and I'll manage."

"Talk about mule-headed, Letti," Alex remonstrat-
ed, "that's the height of it. You get back upstairs and let
me finish this." Taking the fork from the woman's
hand, Alex gave her a gentle push and then turned the
ham.

Letti passed a shaky hand over her wrinkled face.
"Well, in truth, I feel like I've been run over by a herd
of horses. I can't remember when I ever felt worse. If
you're sure you don't mind, I'll mosey back up and
climb into bed."

Alex gave her an understanding pat on the back. "I'll
have your breakfast up in a few minutes, along with a
nice hot cup of coffee."

"Thanks, honey," Letti mumbled hoarsely, dragging
her stout body through the swinging door with a series
of loud sneezes.

Turning back to the stove, Alex stirred the frying
green apples, wiggling her nose delightedly at the sweet
smell of the sugar-coated thin white slices.

"Well, Miss Hawthorne, I didn't know you had
culinary talents."

Alex whipped around to face Damon's smile. "If
you'll wait in the dining room, Damon, I'll get breakfast on the table in just a few minutes. Letti is ill with a
terrible cold and she's gone back to bed."

"Now that's a pity in more ways than one," he
taunted. "I guess we'll all be on a diet around here if
she's sick long."

"I'm a perfectly good cook," Alex retorted crossly.
Wasn't he capable of saying anything nice?

"In the same way that you're a good rider, a good
dancer, and a good driver, Alex?"

Refusing to be baited further, she answered sweetly, "Exactly. But you have no need to fear this morning. Letti had breakfast cooking when I came down. I'm just finishing up."

"I'm glad to hear that." Wiping his brow in feigned relief, he ambled from the kitchen.

Fuming, Alex stood watching the ham fry and the apples simmer until they were done. Struck with a sudden impulse, she removed a portion of the ham and apples for Letti and one for herself and put them on a covered tray with two cups of coffee. Then she left the remainder of the food on the stove, cooking, over a low heat while she started up to Letti's room.

"Be right back to get your breakfast on a plate," she told Damon as she hurried through the dining room.

Without looking up from his paper, he nodded.

"Did you get Damon's breakfast on the table?" Letti asked when Alex had placed the housekeeper's tray on her lap.

"He's reading now," Alex explained truthfully, "but his breakfast will be ready when he is."

Alex stayed long enough to enjoy her own breakfast and to see that Letti ate hers, although the woman confessed to very little appetite. Then she walked unhurriedly back down to the dining room.

Seeing her, Damon shook his head in exasperation. "Well, what about my breakfast?"

"Oh!" she gasped in mock surprise. "I forgot!"

Smiling wickedly to herself, she hurried to the kitchen and looked at the ham, which was now crisp and dry in the middle, the edges almost black. The apples had cooked down to a few assorted peels and a dark bit of ugly, discolored mush.

Quickly, Alex scooped up the entire contents of both pans and dumped them on a plate. Humming a little tune, she sauntered out to the dining room with what was anything but a culinary delight. "Here it is," she proclaimed proudly. Looking just a little sheepish, she added, "It got just a little bit overcooked. I—I hope you don't mind."

In silent horror, Damon stared at the mess. Alex could almost read his mind as she waited for the barb to be unleashed, but it never came. Puzzled, she could only guess that it was too much even for Damon to taunt a woman who cooked so badly.

She sat down with a cheery smile and reached for the paper as Damon gingerly took a fork in hand. "Aren't you going to say grace?" she asked, eyes wide.

The hint of a gleam appeared in his dark eyes. "That, my dear Alex," he murmured quietly, "would be sacrilege."

With the help of several swigs of coffee, somehow Damon managed to consume some of the contents of his plate, and Alex watched with barely suppressed amusement until he finally announced that he could eat no more. Whisking his plate efficiently away, she put the dishes in the dishwasher and then returned to the dining room to find that Damon was ready to go.

They stepped out onto the porch to find a land of white; everything was covered with a blanket of clean snow. George Willis had scraped the driveway and walkway clear, and Damon and Alex were easily able to make their way to the garage. Though the snow was only a few inches deep, it was still slippery and Alex saw that George had put the chains on the blue car.

It was difficult for Alex to remember exactly where she had gone off the road—everything looked so different in the daylight—but Damon went back to the spot where he had picked her up, and they searched from there. About two miles from Willowstone, they saw the Porsche huddled like a hunched-over polar bear under a mound of snow. When they drove past it, Alex exclaimed, "But there it is!"

"Fine," Damon said. "What do you expect me to do about it now?"

"If you intend to leave it there, why did you come to look for it?" she snapped.

He laughed. "When we get home, I'll be able to tell a tow truck driver where it is. You didn't think I'd pull it out of the snow myself, did you?"

She wasn't sure what she had thought, but she couldn't say that to him. "Well, you seemed so concerned about it last night that I wouldn't have been surprised."

"I wasn't concerned about the car itself," he said calmly. "I was concerned that some poor unfortunate driver running unexpectedly into a stalled car in the middle of the road might get himself killed. *That's* why I asked you where it was and if it was completely out of the way."

"Oh," she mumbled. As much as she hated to admit it, it did make sense. She looked out at the snowy countryside, marveling at the breathtaking view. When it became apparent that Damon wasn't going to pursue the subject of the car, Alex took a deep breath and sighed. She was curious about their destination, but if Damon didn't volunteer the information, she was unwilling to ask. She was relieved that she hadn't had to face the ordeal she had anticipated over the car.

Damon drove further out into the country, leaving behind whitened buildings and houses for a lonely road running through dense trees and thick vegetation heavily laden with snow.

"No need to worry," Damon said, giving her a sideways glance. "Snow plows cleared most of these roads early this morning, and the car has snow tires and chains, so we're in no danger."

Alex gazed at him curiously, aware that she had been so entranced by the peaceful scenery that she hadn't thought about the condition of the road. Besides, regardless of whatever else she might think of Damon Montaigne, she was sure that he could handle any emergency. He had long since demonstrated that he bowed not to man, beast, or situation. She smiled a little to herself. Even a woman like Casaundra might find her wings clipped by this powerful figure of a man.

Damon returned the smile he saw on her lips as she looked at him, and Alex couldn't deny that she found him terribly attractive. It was so painful to realize that she was in love with him and that he would never return that love.

"I'm not worried," she said truthfully.

"Good. I love to ride out in the country after a big snowfall. There's something awesome about nature being able to dress the land in pure white."

"It is beautiful," Alex agreed. A steady stream of warm air from the car heater kept her warm and she snuggled against the comfortable seat with an almost visible contentment, unaware that Damon's eyes strayed to her appealing features almost as much as they watched the road.

They turned off the main road onto one even more secluded and winding. Sometime later they stopped before a huge old waterwheel sitting on the edge of a partially frozen stream. An old dilapidated building was beside the wheel, and Alex almost imagined she could see the wheel turning, but of course it was silent and still in the snowy countryside.

Twisting around to look at her, Damon slid his arm across her seat back. "Well, are you getting used to the city again?" he asked. "It's smaller and slower paced than what you've been exposed to, but it does have a certain charm, don't you think?"

"Yes, I do," Alex said quickly. Her heart began to pound and she found herself foolishly tongue-tied in the face of Damon's questions. It was ridiculous, but she wanted him to say that he wanted her to stay in Danville.

"I could operate from one of the larger cities where the schools are located, but I prefer to remain at

home," he remarked. "My Southern roots run deep."
He studied her face for a moment. "However, it's not
my future that's in question, it's yours. And we have to
give it some thought."

Alex nodded, but she didn't want to give any thought
to her future. Not to her career at any rate. Not today.
Not when she was enjoying this special snowy day in
Damon's company. She was suddenly very sorry that
they had started their relationship under such unfortunate circumstances. Had they met at some other time,
perhaps Damon might have come to love her, too. But,
of course, there was still Casaundra; she was the
woman in Damon's life.

Damon watched her for a moment as though he
expected her to say something, and when she didn't, he
turned away from her to start the car. Instead of
returning to Willowstone, he took another isolated
road until they reached an old wooden building. Alex
saw hordes of animals moving about in pens outside
and a sudden burst of pity went through her.

"Oh, look at those poor animals," she murmured
sympathetically. "They must be dreadfully cold
bunched up there in the snow."

"That's why we're here," Damon said. "To look at
them. This is an animal-processing plant."

"An animal-processing plant!" she rasped. "What
are we doing here?"

"You want to be a vet, don't you? This is one of the
things you'll encounter in college. They show you all
sides of the animal business, you know, not just the
pretty ones."

As Alex stared at him, she could feel her face blanch
and her heart begin to pound. She'd die before she
would watch those poor, helpless animals be destroyed;
her heart already ached with pity for them. Somehow
she had to gather the courage to tell Damon that she
had abandoned her plans to be a veterinarian. She had

to, but she wasn't ready for so much unpleasantness just now. She just wasn't prepared—especially after last night. She had wanted to tell him under different circumstances, when she felt more like facing him. She had known it would come to a showdown sooner or later—it had to—but not today.

"Well, don't just sit there, girl," he prompted. "Let's go."

His command reminded her of the day he had left her sitting stupidly on her horse while Casaundra watched, and she hated him afresh. Now he had purposely dragged her to this terrible place without even consulting her, and she had even more reason to despise him. He grabbed her hand, and she tried to yank it free.

"Well, come on. Where's your enthusiasm? You haven't lost it, have you?"

Why couldn't she just admit it? Here was the chance, the opening—but she couldn't do it. "No. Of course not," she snapped, letting him pull her out of the car from his side. She didn't see how she could tell him that she had changed her mind. She would just have to go along with him into the plant. The thought caused her stomach to flip, and her legs suddenly jiggled as she followed uneasily behind him. If she couldn't watch surgery, how could she possibly watch what went on in this place? When they were almost to the door, her shaky legs refused to move forward. She could hear the animals inside, and she turned her head to the side, feeling the tears rush to her eyes. She couldn't go in. She just couldn't! Jerking her hand free of his, she fled back to the security of the car.

She had known a confrontation over her career was coming, but not like this. Not here. Damon had staged it, as he had staged all the other events to show her up. So why, even when she wanted to hate him, almost *did* hate him, did she love him so much? Hastily slipping inside the car, she leaned her head back on the seat, shaking with emotion and disgust. Damon had been right, of course, she would never have made a veterinarian. But he hadn't needed to throw her mistake in her face so savagely. Suddenly she knew that now there was nothing left for her to do but return to California.

Although she didn't look up, she heard Damon enter the car. "Why did you run away?"

She stared straight ahead, eyes unblinking, mouth dry, throat constricted. "I'm not going to be a veterinarian," she answered, dragging each word through her parched lips. There, it was over, said and done. She had admitted she had been wrong. He had been right again.

"What?" he exclaimed. "What did you say?"

She repeated it through tight lips. "I am not going to be a veterinarian."

"Alex, you shock me!" he taunted. "What happened to those dreams?"

"I can't stand to see an animal being operated on," she confessed.

He looked at her curiously for a couple of minutes. "Oh, now I understand," he stated flatly. "Now I see the reason for your hasty interest in Brent. You changed your mind about being a vet, so you decided to go after him as the next best thing. Just like your father, you're bound to chase one foolish dream after another, aren't you? And just like your father, Alex, when you see the going get rough, you run for the easy way out, and you've decided your easy way will be marriage to Brent. Is that it? And what will you do when that fails? Family blood runs deep, doesn't it? You can't look a fact in the face any more than your father could! Alex, you're a quitter, just like he was!"

Without thinking, she lashed out and slapped him cruelly across the face. "Don't you ever say another word to me about my father! Never! Do you hear me? And I'm not going to marry Brent, either, but it wouldn't be any of your business if I was!"

She drew back to hit him again, but having overcome his surprise, Damon was ready for it this time. As her hand came forward, he captured it easily.

"Let me go! Let me go!" she rasped harshly, struggling wildly to free herself.

Damon grabbed both her hands and yanked her across the seat toward him. "Little hellion!" He crushed her to him, putting his lips on hers, punishing her as he ground down on them relentlessly. Alex was left gasping for breath when he freed her, and she swung her hand at him again, but again he stopped her. Tears had welled up in her eyes and threatened to spill down her flaming cheeks.

Damon watched her for a minute. As though purged of his anger by the kiss, he pinned her hands against him and murmured soothingly, "It's all right, Alex. It's all right. You don't have to go to college or marry Brent. I told you before that I had other plans for you. I've set aside an account for you with a generous sum of money in it."

"I don't want your conscience money!" she hissed at him. "I don't want anything of yours. You can't make everything all right with your money! The day I turn twenty-one I'll move out of your house, and I don't want to see you ever again!"

"Oh, Alex," he murmured in a low voice, "there are so many things I could say to you. But it's not the time or the place. I want you to have the money. I put a sum equal to your father's original investment in the account for you when the business started to make money, and I've increased it according to the profits of the other schools. It was my intention to have you attend the business school and take a course in small business management to help me operate the schools. I need help, and I thought you might be interested in the idea, but you wouldn't even listen. You've fought with me every step of the way."

Alex knew there must have been something in the

past that bothered him terribly for him to have put money aside for Allen's child all these years, but she didn't care about that. She didn't want his money. All she had ever wanted from him was his love, she admitted to herself, and now he had hurt her too much for her to want even that. He had played with her feelings, trampled on her dreams, and made a fool of her. She could understand why her father had harbored an undying hatred for the man for so many years. "Just leave me alone."

"Alex, look at me," he demanded. "Your mother knew about my plan and she approved. She wouldn't take any of the money for herself because she respected your father's wishes. He was too full of pride to take a penny of the profits, but she wanted this for you."

Alex turned tearful eyes to him. "I don't know anything about the relationship between you and my mother, but I know my father wouldn't take anything from you and neither will I. I'd rather starve first!"

She saw his jaw muscle begin to twitch, and she turned her head away to stare out at the animals. After what seemed like an eternity, Damon started the car. He drove home in complete silence. When they arrived at Willowstone, she ran up to her room and slammed the door. She didn't come out again until afternoon, and then she took only long enough to check on Letti and make her lunch. She didn't know what Damon ate for lunch, and she didn't care.

When Brent called later in the afternoon, she told him she wasn't free to talk. She didn't care if she never saw Brent again either. She didn't want to think about either man. She shut herself up in her room with a book and tried to blot Damon's face and words from her mind. Dinnertime came before she left her room again. After she had prepared dinner for herself and Letti and had eaten it in Letti's room, she again hid herself away in her own room, punishing her eyes with reading until she couldn't see straight anymore.

It wasn't until she had finally fallen into a deep sleep that she was at peace. Only Damon could grant her real peace, and in her dreams she felt his mouth on hers and once again felt the strength of his powerful arms around her. All thoughts of the miserable day and the bitter words were erased, and she slept soundly through the night.

Chapter Ten

Alex awakened late the next morning. Grateful that it was Sunday and that she had no commitments to keep, she stretched and looked around her room. She thought it would be nice if she could just hide there all day, but with a start she remembered that Letti was ill and might still be lying in bed wanting something to eat. Hopping out of bed, she dressed quickly, taking just a moment to glance out her window to judge the weather. It looked bitterly cold, but it wasn't snowing. Taking Roadside with her, she went to Letti's room and knocked softly. When she received no response, she called out, "Letti? Letti, are you in there?"

Again there was no answer, so she opened the door just enough to see that the bed was properly made before she hurried on her way down the stairs. She was relieved to find that Damon wasn't in the dining room, and she went to the kitchen, where Letti was reading the paper.

"Oh, Letti, you should have gotten me up to fix breakfast this morning," she admonished.

"No. No, child," Letti said. "I feel one hundred percent better today. Matter of fact, after a whole day in bed I'm raring for work. It's against my grain to lollygag around. A waste of time, I always say."

Alex had to smile at the woman. "Yes, I suppose so," she agreed.

"What'll it be for your breakfast? And don't tell me, like Damon did, that you're not hungry. I declare I don't know what's wrong with that man today. As long as I've known him, which is just about all his life, he's only missed breakfast half a dozen times, and that was only when he was really upset over something serious."

"Oh?" Alex was surprised that he ever got terribly upset over anything. She knew he was angry, but she hardly put anger and distress in the same category. "Well, Letti, actually I'm not very hungry this morning either. I think I'll just have some coffee and something sweet."

"Honey, we don't have a single goodie in this house," Letti said, shaking her head. "Yesterday should have been my baking day, and there I was in my bed, lying there like the queen. I suppose I'll do the baking today."

"May I help you?" Alex asked, wanting something to take her mind off her troubles.

"'Course you can, child, if you want to. Maybe today I'll show you how I make my banana-nut bread. It's an old family recipe and real delicious."

"Everything you cook is real delicious," Alex said, teasing a little as she imitated Letti's Southern drawl.

"You're a right good little cook yourself," Letti told her proudly. "When are you going to show Damon?"

Alex flushed. In fact, she never intended to show Damon how well she could cook. In another month she would be twenty-one and would return to California. She felt sure she could find a friend to put her up for a couple of weeks until she could get a job. Her agreement with her mother would have been fulfilled, and she could set about forgetting Damon Montaigne, though she knew in her heart that he was the only man she could ever love. And she wondered why. How could she possibly have fallen in love with such a horrid man?

The snap of Letti's fingers aroused her from her reverie. "I say, child," Letti said with a laugh, "are you sure you're good and awake? Maybe you'd better go back to your bed for a longer snooze."

Alex had to laugh with her. "It does seem that way, doesn't it? I'm afraid my mind was wandering."

"Woolgathering, I always called it," Letti said. "Well, let me get you a nice cup of hot coffee and some cinnamon toast."

"You stay right where you are, Letti. I'll do it myself," Alex insisted, getting a cup.

"I guess you know Damon had the car towed home last evening, don't you?" Letti asked.

Alex stared at her hands. "No, I didn't know. I spent most of the day in my room reading. Was it—is it badly damaged?"

"Not a scratch on the thing. It must have scooted off the road real gentle like, so neither of you was damaged. I guess it got stuck with its tires against one side of the gully, kind of lodged there, but all it got was real muddy."

Alex breathed deeply and expelled her breath slowly. At least Damon wouldn't have a repair bill to add to the amount of money she owed him for the chessmen and Casaundra's dress. "I'm sure glad to hear that," she said, relief evident in her voice.

Damon was gone all day, and Letti and Alex spent the time baking. Letti chattered happily on about local gossip, but Alex listened with only half an ear. She wondered if Damon was still angry with her, and she wondered how he would react when she saw him again.

But she need not have worried. When Damon returned that evening, Casaundra was with him, and he barely acknowledged Alex.

They all dined together. Then Casaundra and

Damon retired to the living room to talk and, Alex thought unhappily, to show their affection for each other in private. With no surprise she realized that she was jealous of the attention Damon gave Casaundra. Alex badly wanted to be in his arms herself. Had she no shame? she wondered. She should despise the man after the things he had said about her and her father. It would be so much easier to hate him for the rest of the time she had to be in his home instead of wishing she were in his arms.

As the days passed, Alex was relieved to find that things fell pretty much into their old routine. Damon spoke civilly to her and watched her with strange, dark eyes when she was in his company, but he made no further remarks about either her past or her future. Her life seemed to be in limbo as far as he was concerned. She found that Tuesday came around regrettably fast, and she had to decide whether or not to continue working with Brent at the clinic. As much as she hated to face him after all the things that had happened, she knew she would need money to return to California. But she also knew she wouldn't go out with him again. She couldn't bear his arms about her when Damon was the man she loved.

Tuesday morning she slid into coffee-colored slacks and a tangerine sweater and slipped down the stairs for breakfast. When she found Damon sitting at the table, she knew she couldn't avoid a conversation; she needed to know if he would allow her to drive the Porsche again. She decided it would be safer to ask for one of the other cars, but she waited until Letti came in to inquire about her breakfast before she got up the courage to ask.

"Perhaps you would rather I drove the blue car to work today, Damon, instead of the Porsche," she blurted out, taking the bull by the horns and trying to sound as if there was no reason why she shouldn't drive one of his cars.

When he looked up from his newspaper, Alex wished she hadn't asked. The dark eyes searched her face as if he couldn't believe her gall, but then she discovered a glint of amusement in them. "You mean you're giving me an option on which of my automobiles you wreck next?"

Alex couldn't miss the mocking look on his face, and her old anger surged afresh. "I don't want to seem to be partial to any one car in particular," she flashed in irritation.

She was rewarded with a big smile, and she was unable to resist thinking that he really was the most handsome man she had ever seen. Then she remembered that he was playing with her again, and she should be hating him.

"Drive whichever one you want. However, I've gotten rather used to driving the Ford myself. I'd hate to see it in a gully. It's been so reliable. The Porsche seems more your kind of car."

"Thank you," she returned icily, but she was surprised that it seemed as if nothing had changed between them, regardless of how topsy-turvy her heart had been in the past few days.

Alex entered the clinic reluctantly and Ruth, unaware of her disastrous Friday night, greeted her warmly.

"Did you get home all right Friday night? I missed you Saturday but Doc said you were okay—just taking a day off to be with Damon."

Trying to smile, Alex nodded. "Yes, I got home." But she thought, So that was what Damon had told Brent! And if Brent loved her as he had said, why hadn't he at least asked to speak to her?

When she found the examination room empty, she

remembered that this was a surgery day. She hated surgery days most of all and, as she went back to the operating room, she promised herself that she would take a job as a secretary when she returned to California. The irony of it caused her to laugh aloud, and Brent, glancing up to acknowledge her presence, stared at her oddly. "Good morning, Alex," he said, and Alex thought his cheeks turned a little pink.

"Good morning."

With no mention of Friday night, he asked. "Ready for work? We missed you around here on Saturday."

Even though Alex was relieved that he wasn't professing his love for her again, she was shocked almost speechless at his nonchalance. He spoke to her as if she were just like any other employee. She was incredulous, wondering what Damon had said to him that caused him to change so suddenly. It was another reminder of how the powerful Mr. Montaigne browbeat his companions until they bowed to his wishes. Well, she told herself, if Brent could be knocked down that easily, she didn't want him anyway. But she had known that already. She was determined, however, not to be under Damon's thumb herself. The whole situation was just one more reason to return to California. California—it seemed so long ago that it had been her home.

"Alex, are you ready?" Brent repeated in a very professional voice.

"Yes. Yes, I am," she murmured, turning her attention to the task at hand. Somehow the day passed.

Like the quickly melting snow, one day blended into another, and Alex found that life had become routine again. March, with its blustery winds and new beginnings, settled on the town. The flowers began to wake from their long sleep, and the trees started into new life with shoots and green leaves. Damon and Alex had an uneasy truce with each other. Alex didn't tell him that she was planning to go back to California in April, and he didn't discuss her career plans. He seemed to have washed his hands of her future.

Brent no longer asked her out, and as puzzled as she was over his fizzled passion, she didn't have the nerve to ask Damon what he'd said, nor the inclination to ask Brent what had happened for fear of reawakening his interest. She was spending time with Ruth, and she was enjoying the friendship. She was also getting very good at chess, but she doubted that she would ever use her skills with Damon.

Damon seemed to be seeing a lot of Casaundra, or maybe he had always spent a lot of time with her and Alex was just beginning to realize it because Casaundra was at Willowstone more often. On numerous occasions the woman simply dropped by unannounced, but Damon was always glad to see her.

The school in New York was almost ready to open, and Casaundra was going there for two months to set things up until they found someone suitable to replace her. In the meantime, they needed someone to manage the local school, and now Alex could understand what Damon had meant when he told her he needed help. As it was, he would have to spend a lot of time at the local school even if Casaundra could find a manager willing to work for only two months. Alex decided it really wasn't any of her business, but in the past Damon had tried to involve her, and she did have a workable idea. As she listened to them go over the problem for the third time at the dinner table, she timidly offered a suggestion.

"Why not," she asked, "find someone who is willing to relocate to work the two months in the established operation here, learning your methods, while Casaundra sets up the New York school, and then have that person take over the New York school?"

Staring at her with surprise in his eyes, Damon didn't say anything for a few seconds. Alex wondered why she hadn't just kept her mouth shut.

Casaundra pursed her lips as if to tell Alex to mind her own business, and Alex, embarrassed, shifted her eyes to Letti, who beamed brightly at her.

"Why not indeed?" Damon exclaimed at length. "That's such a simple solution! I can't imagine why we didn't think of it ourselves, Casaundra."

"It was so simple that it went right over our heads," Casaundra replied in a surly voice.

"I always did think you would have your father's brains for business organization, Alex," Damon remarked, a smile tugging the corners of his mouth.

Alex returned the smile. At least he had admitted that she and her father were capable in some area.

"Well, I have to go," Casaundra said, getting up from the table. "See me to the door, Damon."

A day later, the day before Casaundra was to leave for New York, she stopped by again. Since she always seemed to know when Damon was home, it was strange for her to turn up on a day when he was absent, and, seeing her car from the window, Alex assumed that she must have come to pick up some business-related material.

She heard the doorbell ring, but, knowing Letti would answer it—and preferring to miss Casaundra's call, she remained in her room. Again the bell sounded impatiently, and Alex sighed as she went to answer it. Apparently Letti was occupied elsewhere. Smoothing down the plain little brown dress she wore, Alex hurried to the stairway.

When she saw Letti coming out of the kitchen wiping flour on her apron, she stopped at the top of the stairs. "Will you get it, Alex?" Letti called up. "I'm right in the middle of making pie dough."

Alex smiled affectionately at the woman. She would miss her when she left Willowstone. "Sure, you go back to your pies. And Letti," she added, "bake an apple one for me."

Letti smiled agreeably at her.

With a long exasperated buzz, the doorbell sounded again. "It's Casaundra," Alex explained. "I saw her car from my window."

Letti scowled as she turned back toward the kitchen. "Better you than me," she muttered.

Reluctantly, Alex went to the door.

The faintest flicker of disdain passed over Casaundra's face as she stood on the front porch tapping the fingers of one hand on the edge of her purse. "Well, do I have to stand here all day, Alex? Or will you let me come inside?"

"Oh, I am sorry," Alex said without sincerity as she opened the door wide. Casaundra immediately swept in as if she were mistress of the house.

"Damon isn't home, Casaundra."

"Oh, he isn't?" Casaundra's face wore an odd expression.

"No."

"How long do you expect him to be gone?"

"I don't really know. He doesn't inform me of his plans," Alex admitted.

"No, I guess he wouldn't," Casaundra purred.

Alex knew the statement was meant to put her in her place and she bristled at it. "Well, what do you want, Casaundra?"

"Damon." The word rolled smoothly off Casaundra's tongue. "But since he isn't home, I'll just wait. Perhaps he won't be gone too long."

Alex had hoped she wouldn't want to wait, but because she did Alex had no choice but to entertain her for the sake of politeness. "Fine," she agreed halfheartedly, wishing she could walk away coldly, leaving the woman standing there in the hall.

"Thank you." Casaundra's voice was exaggerated in its gratitude.

Sweeping down the hallway on high heels, her rose skirt hugging her full hips, Casaundra flounced past Alex as if Alex were the housemaid. As she marched into the living room, she flung her purse down on the settee before seating herself comfortably. She looked very much at home. Almost, Alex thought ruefully, as if she belonged there, and she had to force herself to follow Casaundra into the room.

Alex seated herself in the beige chair. "Would you like some coffee?" she asked, making a decided effort to remain civil to the other woman.

"Where's Letti?" The question was more of a demand than an inquiry.

"She's in the kitchen making pies. I'll get the coffee," Alex answered, biting her tongue to keep the bitterness out of her voice.

A glint of determination gleamed in Casaundra's cool violet eyes. "I don't want any coffee. I want to talk."

Alex looked at her, puzzled. She shrugged her shoulders. "What do you want to talk about?"

"Just what are your plans, Alex?" Casaundra asked bluntly. "Damon tells me you're no longer interested in the vet field, and Brent tells me you're no longer interested in him. Just what is it you *are* interested in?"

Alex stifled her irritation. "Really, Casaundra, I don't see that my future plans are any of your business. They hardly concern you," she replied firmly.

Instantly, Casaundra's eyes blazed. "Well, now that's where you're mistaken. They certainly do concern me, and I'm making it plain to you right now—Damon is mine. Keep away from him!"

"What on earth are you talking about?" Alex asked, astonished at the woman's outburst.

"Don't pretend with me," Casaundra snapped vehemently. "Your mother's plans to get Damon for herself failed, but even in death she doesn't give up, does she?" Her laughter was short and bitter. "Ten years later she sends you with the same purpose—to take my man! Well, it won't work!"

"You're lying!" Alex accused, shock whitening her face. "My mother was never interested in Damon! She couldn't have been!"

Casaundra stood up and glared at Alex. "You stupid little fool! Why do you think your father rushed off to California with the two of you in tow? Because he caught your mother with Damon, that's why!"

Alex shook her head in denial, refusing to believe the woman's ugly accusation. "You're making that up! My mother loved my father."

Casaundra smiled wickedly. "Did she? Then why was she so interested in Damon? It never bothered her at all that he was seven years younger than she was or that she was a married woman. She was always wanting to see him on some pretense or another. And I should know. I heard Damon talking to her on the phone that last time. I heard him tell her where to meet him, but I fixed both of them. I told Allen!"

Alex could feel her heart racing and there was a tenseness in the pit of her stomach. She stared into Casaundra's hateful eyes. "I don't believe a word of this!"

"I don't care whether you believe it or not, it's still true. Ask anyone in town! Everyone knew about Lena and Damon. And now *you're* here, just like Lena wanted, following right in her footsteps. I dare you to deny that you want Damon for yourself!"

Alex shook her head and blinked her eyelids against the building tears. Her mother and Damon! So this was the dirty little secret that everyone had hinted at! And Casaundra was right! She *had* followed right in her mother's footsteps. She was in love with Damon, too!

Casaundra's enraged face was triumphant. "You can't deny it, can you? You love the man! I won't stand by and see Damon fall for another Hawthorne woman! He's mine and I intend to keep him!"

Alex stood up, almost blinded by her tears. "Don't worry, Casaundra," she said bitterly, "I don't want Damon Montaigne!" Then she turned on her heel and fled from the room. But what she had said was a lie. She wanted Damon more than anything in the world. She knew that she had to leave Willowstone, and she had to leave it immediately. She couldn't stay under Damon's roof another night. Damon and her mother!

She stumbled up the steps and ran to her room to drag out her old suitcase. Slamming it down on the bed, she began to shove her clothes into it. She would have to leave her books and other odds and ends behind, and she would have to leave Roadside, but it couldn't be helped. When the suitcase was crammed full of her belongings, she hurried to the old desk and quickly scrawled a note to Letti, telling her that Damon could pick up his car at the airport and saying that she was going back to California and would get in touch with Letti later. But Alex didn't know if she would ever contact the old housekeeper again. She couldn't risk letting Damon know where she was. She must never see him again and she certainly didn't want to hear anything about him. Her heart couldn't stand it.

Pulling her coat from the closet, she threw it around her shoulders and picked up her purse and the suitcase. She had no idea when a plane would be leaving Danville, but she would make the first connection she could and transfer somewhere along the way to get to California. She couldn't delay a moment; she had to leave Willowstone—and Damon—today.

Glancing down the hall to be sure that Letti was still in the kitchen, Alex quickly made her way out to the car. Blindly, she tossed the suitcase into the trunk and slid in behind the wheel. Scarcely noting that Casaundra had left, Alex started the car and drove down the driveway. Then the tears began to stream down her cheeks. How could her mother have deceived her so? How could she have deceived Alex's father so?

She didn't know how, but she finally managed to find the airport and park the car. Hastily jerking the luggage from the trunk, she closed the lid, then ran toward the terminal. She had almost reached the door when she stopped. For a moment she was sure her ears were deceiving her; she thought she heard those heavy, ominous footsteps that she had heard so often recently—Damon's footsteps—but, of course, he couldn't know that she was running away. Nevertheless, she was forced to turn around to see who was behind her, and she gasped as she stared up into Damon's dark eyes.

Rapidly closing the gap between them, he spun her around and demanded, "What on earth do you think you're doing?"

She tried to meet his hard stare, but she couldn't. Averting her eyes, she murmured, "I'm going back to California."

"Why?" he demanded. "Letti found your note and called me, but it was hardly adequate to explain why you're sneaking off like this."

Alex felt a sob catch in her throat and her lips were parched when she tried to speak. What could she possibly say? Shaking her head helplessly, she turned away again and started to flee. But he quickly thwarted her escape.

"Damn you, Alex," he muttered, grabbing her wrist and causing her to lose her grip on the suitcase, "don't you run out on me. I asked you a question. Why are you leaving?"

Alex raised tearful blue eyes to meet the cold brown of his. "Casaundra told me about—about—" The words stuck in her throat. "She told me about you and my mother."

"She told you *what*?" Damon snarled, his brows creasing in anger.

Alex lowered her eyes. She was ashamed and humiliated that she should be in love with her mother's lover. She felt betrayed and embarrassed by her mother's behavior, and she felt very sorry for her father. "Why, Damon?" she asked through trembling lips. "Why didn't you tell me about my mother? That's why my father hated you, isn't it? That's why you had me come here." Blue eyes brilliant with tears searched his handsome face. "Well, you might have owed my father something, but you owe me nothing." Her voice was ragged. "Now, please, let me go. I don't ever want to see you again."

Damon grasped her chin in his hand and tipped her head back so that she was forced to look into his eyes. "What are you talking about? What did Casaundra tell you?"

Alex choked back bitter tears. Damon obviously wanted her humiliation to be complete. He wanted her to have to state the awful truth herself. "That you and my mother were lovers. Isn't that enough?"

Holding her chin securely, Damon forced her to look into his eyes. "Alex, it wasn't that way. I never had an affair with your mother. She was devoted to your father. The business was failing and Allen was about to fall apart. Your mother and I were good friends— nothing more. She called me in tears that day, saying that she had to talk to me about Allen. She said he was so depressed that he was drinking and unmanageable. I agreed to meet her at a small cafe to talk." He drew a deep breath as though the memory of that day still troubled him. "Your father showed up, not quite sober, mad as the devil, and he accused us of all kinds of things. None of them were true, of course. The next day he demanded his share of the profits from the school and left with you two for California."

Alex looked into the depths of Damon's eyes and she knew that he was telling the truth. "Casaundra," she whispered. "Casaundra told my father about the meeting between you and my mother. She told me so."

Damon's face registered shock. "Casaundra told you that?"

Alex nodded.

"Casaundra," Damon groaned. "Why? I never had any idea she was behind it."

"You should have," Alex accused bitterly, freeing her chin from his hand. "You're not blind. You must have known she was in love with you! She still is."

"Casaundra and I have never been anything more than good friends and business associates. She knew there couldn't be anything more. I was never in love with her. We talked about it when she and Brent broke up. I have a great respect for her business skills—she's been a tremendous asset—but I never offered her anything more than a job."

Alex blinked wide blue eyes. "But she—but Brent thought—I thought—oh, you've been so cruel to me," she finished lamely.

"I haven't been cruel to you, Alex. You've fought me every inch of the way. When your mother called and told me she was dying and that she was worried about you and what would become of you, I wanted to make up in some way for the unhappiness I'd inadvertently caused your family. I'll admit that I was expecting a young girl—your mother said you were a lot like Allen in your ideals—and I still thought of you as the child who went to California. I wasn't prepared for a beautiful, headstrong young woman who was obviously bent on revenge for some imagined injustice done to her father. I told myself that you were just a confused young girl, but I was attracted to you immediately. Oh, Alex," he groaned suddenly, "don't you know how I've wanted you?"

Alex's eyes met his again, and she felt her pounding heart skip a beat. Was it possible that he really cared for her?

"I didn't want to be attracted to you," he said in a hoarse voice. "When you accused me of sending for you for some twisted, less than honorable reason I felt incredibly guilty. It was all I could do that first night I saw you standing before me barely clothed not to wrap my arms around you. I knew I was out of line for wanting you, and I didn't know what to do about it. It was obvious that you wanted to hate me. I knew you needed time to adjust, but every time I touched you, my soul flamed. I tried to resist you, but, heaven help me, I *did* want you for myself. And being around you all the time, I couldn't help falling in love with you. When I saw Brent at the dance with you, I wanted to strangle him—and you, too."

"Then you're the reason he suddenly lost interest in me," she exclaimed.

"Yes," he agreed. "Alex, I have no excuses for my behavior except that I love you. I know this is sudden, and I don't expect you to give me your answer right now, but I want to marry you."

Alex opened her mouth to speak, but Damon silenced her with a finger to her lips. "Sh. Don't refuse me yet. I know how you feel about a career, and about me, but I love you. I want you to think about it, Alex."

Overcome with happiness, tears slipped from Alex's eyes and she shook her head in wonder. "Oh, Damon, I don't have to think about it. I love you. I just never dared to dream that you loved me, too."

Surprise transformed Damon's face. "How could you not have seen the love I felt for you? Every time we touched, I ached to hold you in my arms. Good heavens, woman! You should have known that only a man in love could have eaten that breakfast you served me. If you say yes to my proposal, Letti will have to teach you to cook."

A gentle laugh escaped Alex's lips and she blushed. "I can cook perfectly well, Damon."

Momentary confusion showed on his face before dark brows drew menacingly together. "Then tell me, little girl—how do you explain that disastrous meal you served me?" A knowing look flashed into his dark eyes.

"Alex," he growled, "you didn't deliberately burn my breakfast!"

Pink flames danced on her cheeks and she inclined her head. "Yes, I did. But you asked for it! You were so sure that I couldn't do anything right that I couldn't bear to disappoint you!"

A smile played on his lips before Damon laughed deeply. "Alex, you really are a little hellion—my little hellion. I wouldn't want you any other way. You're woman enough for any man. Come on, we're going home."

Alex considered his words for a moment and she knew she really was going home. Home to Willowstone and her destiny. She raised laughing blue eyes to meet warm brown ones and Damon's lips blotted out all other thoughts as they descended to hers—claiming, caressing, calling for her love.

Silhouette Romance

15-Day Free Trial Offer
6 Silhouette Romances

6 Silhouette Romances, free for 15 days! We'll send you 6 new Silhouette Romances to keep for 15 days, absolutely free! If you decide not to keep them, send them back to us. We'll pay the return postage. You pay nothing.

Free Home Delivery. But if you enjoy them as much as we think you will, keep them by paying us the retail price of just $1.50 each. We'll pay all shipping and handling charges. You'll then automatically become a member of the Silhouette Book Club, and will receive 6 more new Silhouette Romances every month and a bill for $9.00. That's the same price you'd pay in the store, but you get the convenience of home delivery.

Read every book we publish. The Silhouette Book Club is the way to make sure you'll be able to receive every new romance we publish.

This offer expires October 31, 1981

Silhouette Book Club, Dept. SBC17B
120 Brighton Road, Clifton, NJ 07012

Please send me 6 Silhouette Romances to keep for 15 days, absolutely free. I understand I am not obligated to join the Silhouette Book Club unless I decide to keep them.

NAME

ADDRESS

CITY   STATE   ZIP

Silhouette Romance

ROMANCE THE WAY
IT USED TO BE...
AND COULD BE AGAIN

Contemporary romances for today's women.

Each month, six very special love stories will be yours

from SILHOUETTE.

Look for them wherever books are sold

or order now from the coupon below.

$1.50 each

Silhouette Romance

Coming in June From Silhouette

JANET DAILEY'S
THE HOSTAGE BRIDE

- -